"NOW, LEE," DAVE SAID QUIETLY

He dived to his left, plucking out the heavy gun as he moved. He knew that the pistol was so powerful it could break his wrist if he wasn't properly braced to fire it. The snow erupted behind him as the silent member of the quartet triggered both barrels of his ten-gauge. From inside the tent there was the lighter crack of the Beretta, followed by a scream. And there was the unmistakable snarling of Melmoth in a fury.

Lee had let go of the pit bull as soon as he heard his father say the code word "accident." Gripping the scattergun to his shoulder, he allowed the muzzle to protrude an inch through the tent flap. He took a slow breath and held it. Like his father, he couldn't believe he was actually going to shoot at another human being.

At his father's command, Lee squeezed the trigger, feeling the buck of the gun against his shoulder, seeing his target go down, thrashing on the ground and yelping in pain. At that same moment the bottom of the tent flap flew outward and Melmoth was in the open, racing toward the short blond man.

James McPhee

SURVIVAL 2000

BLOOD QUEST

A GOLD EAGLE BOOK FROM

WORLDWIDE.

TORONTO • NEW YORK • LONDON • PARIS
AMSTERDAM • STOCKHOLM • HAMBURG
ATHENS • MILAN • TOKYO • SYDNEY

This is for everyone in the
Art Department at Gold Eagle, who
consistently turn covers into gold.
With sincere thanks.

First edition February 1991

ISBN 0-373-63201-0

BLOOD QUEST

Many say that the darkest hour is that which comes just before dawn. I say they are wrong. There are those of us who find the dark on dark that follows the dawning is the bleakest time of all.

—*Deserts of Vast Eternity*
by Lloyd Thursby, Weyman Press
New Brunswick, 1968

1

From 6 November 2048 issue of the Drowned Creek Picayune and Weekly Advertiser, *Colorado.*

HEAD FOR HILLS
SAYS LOCAL STAR-SPOTTER

Sky watcher Harry Engelbrecht of Box Canyon Road has a warning for all the good folk who read the *Picayune*. Mr. Engelbrecht has been a keen astronomer since his teens, and a couple of nights ago his big lens picked out something a bit unusual. The father of three, Harry was searching the area between Mars and Jupiter when he saw something he didn't much like.

It was a rogue planet, spinning through space, and according to garage mechanic Harry, it's coming OUR way!

So, make sure you carry your umbrella with you, friends, before it starts raining meteors.

Don't want you seeing stars!

Remember, you read it first in the *Picayune*.

2

Melmoth, the crossbred pit bull, bellied down in the snow, snarling a warning.

"Someone coming, Dad," said Lee Rand quietly. "From the north, sounds like."

His father nodded. "Be the ones we heard shooting last evening. Best be ready."

It was 4 July 2050. Dave and Lee Rand were sharing Independence Day together in what had once been the Cibola National Forest, fifty miles west of Socorro, New Mexico. For the first time in several weeks, the sky was mainly blue, the temperature just before noon climbing close to freezing.

They'd picked a camp site with a good outlook, on a ridge protruding above the snow-tipped pines around them. As soon as Melmoth began to give warning, Dave had stamped out the smoldering remnants of their night fire with a hissing of embers in the trampled snow.

"First time the sun's been through in a few weeks," said Lee.

"You remember camping here in '47? Your mother and the girls were all here that time. We had the van, as well. Melmoth was only a puppy. You remember it?"

"Sure. I got poison ivy real bad."

Dave nodded. "Yeah. It was late July then. Daytime temperature never dipped under eighty. Boy..." His voice trailed away as he stared out over the whited land, recalling what it had been like back then. Three whole years ago. "A lifetime," he said quietly.

The dog was standing erect now, muscled shoulders braced, hair prickling along his spine. The jaws were partly open, and a thread of saliva trickled between the strong teeth into the powdered snow between the front paws. The slit eyes looked fixedly toward the north, in the direction of the abandoned township of Magdalena.

"Sure is something," Dave said. "Best get ourselves ready."

THE PATCHED Aerolyte Wilderness double tent had its flap tied shut. Lee was inside, holding Melmoth by the heavy studded collar, keeping the animal quiet with a warning hand on its tapered muzzle. His beloved Beretta Onyx scattergun was cradled in the boy's arms, cocked and ready. The weapon had belonged to his grandfather and had been a gift on Lee's thirteenth birthday. It had been one of the things he'd brought along on their winter camping vacation. A vacation that had already lasted the better part of eighteen months. The SIG-Sauer 232 was in the hip holster, a spare mag for it on one of the lightweight sleeping bags.

The 9 mm handgun hadn't been included at the start of their trip.

Nor had some of the other weapons that they'd acquired in the past year and a half. The idea of going backpacking with a machine pistol, two hunting rifles, a pair of longbows, two shotguns and three handguns would have been totally absurd.

"Better be safe," whispered the boy, repeating one of his father's favorite sayings. So far they'd been safe. But from things that they'd seen in the past year and a half, Lee also guessed they'd been lucky.

Melmoth growled deep in his belly. It was so low a sound that the boy could feel it vibrate through the pit bull's body rather than actually hear it.

Lee shuffled a little nearer to the flap of the tent, squinting through a narrow gap. Now he could hear the faint noise of boots crunching in powdery snow.

"Hello the camp! Four of us out here. All right if'n we come nearer?"

The voice was light and friendly. Lee tightened his grip on the dog's muzzle, feeling the first feather-touch of fear.

Dave Rand stood by the remains of the fire, his back to the tent to leave a clear field of vision to-ward the track where the men had appeared. This was the moment he'd been anticipating through the long months of isolation in the backcountry. The months without sight of another human being, keeping away from the different shades of madness that ran foaming through the land like a red tide. It was the moment that he'd tried to pre-pare his son for, and now it could be upon them.

"Come ahead a few steps, slow and easy. Ap-preciate it if you could keep your hands out in plain sight for me."

Four men, shrouded in heavy coats of fur and leather. Two of them had skis strapped across their shoulders. All wore gun belts over their coats, and two had either rifles or shotguns in their hands. The unusual sunlight, bright off the snow, made it difficult to see. They were around thirty yards away from Dave Rand.

They shuffled toward him, slow and cautious, stopping twenty paces off. Their spokesman was bearded, his jacket dull plaid. Dave had been a keen member of the shooting club back in Cody Heights. Back home, a few miles from Bakersfield, in California. Seven hundred miles and a lifetime away. Now that they were a little closer, he recognized most of the hardware toted by the quartet of strangers.

Browning Hi-Power for the leader. Small Heckler & Koch P9B to the skinny man on the right. An Astra A95 for the stocky figure on the farther end of the line. He couldn't make out the other pistol for certain, but it looked like a nickelplated heavy-caliber revolver. Maybe an old Smith & Wesson 625-2.

"You up here all on your ownsome, mister?" Almost imperceptibly the four men were fanning out.

Dave licked his lips, tasting the salve he'd put on after breakfast that morning. The strangers hadn't actually done anything threatening, yet he could feel his heart beating a touch faster.

"Yeah. Live in Albuquerque. I'm an accountant." He managed a laugh. "Guess I don't do much these days. The Big One sort of killed off trade for me. Been hunting up here."

The skinny man pushed back his hood, showing a shock of corn blond hair. The barrel of his

10-gauge was easing toward Dave. "Hear there's deer in the forest. We got us one 'bout a week ago. What you caught, mister?"

"Few rabbits."

The leader spoke again, pointing at the gun on Dave's hip. "Shoot them with that cannon, did you? Can't have been much left but bone splinters and a splash of blood. What the hell sort of pistol is it?"

"Four seventy-five Linebaugh. Built on a Ruger Bisley Blackhawk frame."

"Four seventy-five! Holy shit! You could knock the head off a grizzly with a gun like that. Mind if I look at it?"

The bearded man took another couple of casual steps forward, his hand stretched out.

In their repeated talks about just such an eventuality, Dave and Lee had agreed upon a variety of code words. Sitting alone round a bright fire, it hadn't seemed that serious to either of them.

"Hold it there," said Dave, dropping his hand to the butt of the Linebaugh. "Wouldn't want an accident."

"Accident" was one of the words they'd agreed on. It meant that the situation was potentially very serious and that Lee should ready himself to take unilateral action.

"Won't be no fucking accident, mister," snarled the blond man. "Not less'n you're more fucking stupid than you look."

"Harvey's right, mister. Leave that big old gun be where it is."

Dave Rand couldn't believe what was happening. Many times over the past months he'd wondered if he'd become trapped in a living nightmare, or whether his work had got on top of him and he'd suffered some kind of bizarre breakdown. Now this. Four men, heavily armed, threatening him with violence. With death.

He kept his hand where it was, feeling the coolness of the polished walnut butt of the Linebaugh. "You men should keep on moving."

His voice cracked, thin and reedy, and he could hear with self-contempt the middle-class tone. As if he was warning some hobo to get out of his swimming pool.

The men laughed. One of them parodied his voice, placing a mincing hand on hip. "Oh, dear, we men sure should keep moving or he'll set the cops on us." He spit in the snow. The humor disappeared. "Let's fucking get to it, Harry."

"Now, Lee," said Dave quietly.

He dived to his left, plucking out the heavy gun as he moved, knowing that the pistol was so pow-

erful that it could break his wrist if he wasn't
properly braced to fire it. The snow erupted behind him as the silent member of the quartet
snapped off both barrels of his 10-gauge. The air
seemed filled with noise and smoke and shouts.
From inside the tent there was the lighter crack of
the Beretta, followed by a scream.

And there was the unmistakable snarling of
Melmoth in a fury.

Lee had let go of the pit bull as soon as he heard
his father say the codeword "accident." Gripping
the scattergun to his shoulder, allowing the muzzle to protrude an inch through the tent flap, he
drew a bead on the knees of the leader of the
foursome. He took a slow breath and held it; like
his father, he was unable to truly believe he was
actually going to shoot at another human being.

At his father's command, he squeezed the trigger, feeling the bucking of the stock against his
shoulder, seeing his target go down, thrashing in
the snow and yelping in pain. At that same moment the bottom of the tent flap burst open and
Melmoth was already bounding outside, heading
for the short blond man.

A rifle barked, and Dave Rand had no idea
where the bullet had gone. He'd rolled into the
classic prone shooter's position, the gun extended

in front of him, his right hand supported by his left. Drawing a bead on the man with the smoking shotgun, he pulled on the trigger.

He knew what the kick was like. Even knew the ballistics that lay behind it. The Linebaugh fired a 440-grain bullet on maximum charge at over thirteen hundred feet per second. That was a recoil energy figure in excess of fifty foot pounds. Just about the same as simultaneously firing *four* cartridges from a .44 Magnum!

All of that sped through his mind as he absorbed the short sharp kick. Seeing the man he'd aimed at go flying backward as if someone had hooked his collar from behind, Dave shifted smoothly along, just as if he were still in the butts at Cody Heights. Centering the post foresight on the next man along, who had dodged sideways and was now crouching, his rifle leveled at the tent.

Dave fired a second shot, blinking at the illusion that the kneeling man's head had turned into a melon that had been pulped by an invisible hammer. It wasn't like target practice. And it wasn't like the war-vids Ellie liked to watch.

It was much less real than any of that.

He was ready to fire again, with three rounds remaining in the handgun. But there wasn't anything left for him to shoot at.

The headless man was kicking and thrashing like a beginner in the shallow end. The man who'd fired the shotgun had disappeared completely, his body thrown down the slope of the path among the trees. The leader of the attack was lying on his side, knees drawn up, clutching at his bloodied legs. His guns were both fallen in the snow, several feet away from him. And the fourth man, the blonde, had stopped crying out for help, concentrating his efforts on keeping Melmoth's teeth away from his throat. From what Dave could see, it was a losing struggle.

Lee pushed his head out of the tent, his face white as parchment, holding the Beretta in front of him as though it were an icon to ward off evil.

"Dad?"

"Here, Lee. It's all right. Check out the guy over the hill." Then, lifting his voice, he added, "And be careful."

He stood up, adopting the sort of pose that he remembered from the cop shows—drawing a bead on the man shot through both knees, also watching the fight between Melmoth and the shortest of the four.

"Get him off, mister! For Christ's sake . . ."

There was no way at all that David Alexander Rand, accountant from Cody Heights, California, could just stand there while his dog butchered a human being. No way at all.

Not then.

"Melmoth! Leave him!"

But the pit bull had tasted blood, sensing the threat of violence against its two masters. It wasn't about to stop just because it vaguely heard, through the roaring crimson fog, its own name being called out.

Dave stepped in close, holding the heavy pistol in his right hand, snatching at the dog's collar with his left hand and heaving it away, its front legs scraping the air, bloody foam clotting around its panting jaws. For a moment he thought he might have to club the animal to the ground, but he shouted its name again, jerking its collar and eventually bringing sense back.

"Sit! Sit there, Melmoth!" he yelled, risking letting go.

The dog slowly lowered itself, eyes never leaving the weeping man lying in the red-smeared snow.

"Dad!"

"What?"

Lee was standing over the other attacker, keeping the Beretta on him. "Other two are real dead. One's got no head..." For a moment Dave thought his son was going to pass out. "The other's got a hole in his chest you could drive a semi through."

"Jesus, mister! We didn't mean no harm. Wanted some food. Food's all."

Dave stared down into the puckered face of the straw-headed man. Hardly recognizable for the gashes and bruising where Melmoth had got through at his face and throat. But it didn't look like any of the wounds would prove fatal. From where he stood, Dave could also see the effect of the shotgun on the leader. His jeans were stripped off, and there was nothing but pulped flesh at both knees, with the whiteness of bone.

"Mister! Let us go, huh? We didn't want to do no hurt."

"Lying bastard!"

Keeping an eye on the crippled man, Lee edged over to join his father. His face was pale, and he kept licking his lips. Dave realized the boy was barely holding off tears.

"What're we gonna do, Dad? That guy can't walk. He'll die if we leave him."

Dave nodded, locked into his own thoughts and memories.

Three years ago ... Christ, was that only three years ago? An Easter vacation. Near Canyon de

Chelly. All five of them. Young woman riding a big old Harley bike had lost it on a rain-slick curve. They'd been first on the scene. Janine had driven for help with the girls. Lee had stayed with him while he cradled the dying girl in his arms. Trying to comfort her, ease the lonely agony of her passing. He would never forget seeing the life go from the blue eyes and the face become dull flesh. That had been about the worst moment of his entire life.

"Leave them," he said.

"Dad..."

"Now's not the time for this, son. But they came here to kill me. You, too. And Melmoth. Steal what they wanted. This isn't a damned game, Lee. You should know that by now."

"We got no food, mister."

The leader had passed out. Blood was leaking from his wounds at such a rate that Dave figured he wouldn't make it through another hour.

Dave realized with something of a shock that the man on the ground in front of him was probably no older than eighteen. Tears were mingling with the blood washing down on the soft face.

"We'll leave you a couple of tins of ham we got. That's all."

"It won't last us long," the blond one whined.

Dave holstered the Linebaugh, finding his own fingers were trembling. "All you get. Don't push it. Your friend there won't need any."

"He's my daddy. Other two were his brothers. We been hunting these parts ever since It hit."

Dave shook his head. "Watch him, Lee. Careful. I'll pack up the tent."

The blond boy moved as if he was going to get up. Melmoth raised himself and growled, low and menacing.

"Best keep still," warned Lee.

"Sure, sure."

BY THE TIME they were ready to move, everything backpacked, the older man was dead. Dave left the canned meat and a can of peach slices by the son, who ignored him.

Lee looked at his father expectantly. "Where we going?"

Dave looked toward the west. "I thought we might try home," he said.

3

From 11 November 2048 issue of the Los Angeles Globe, *an item in the "Here, There & Everywhere" section.*

A local paper up in affluent Colorado tells us about one Harry Engelbrecht, an amateur astronomer and part-time prophet of doom.

Seems he spotted something big and unpleasant heading straight toward us. No, it wasn't another hunk of sugar-rock from Sukie Wolfff. It's a rogue planet, coming earthward.

We've checked with our own *Globe* starwatcher, and he tells us that it's all in the mind. Or in the eye. He contacted local skyspotters, and nobody else seems to have seen this cosmic threat.

So, maybe the Planet Engelbrecht has vanished into its own black hole.

Like Elisha Cook Junior once said in some old movie: "Keep watching the skies!"

4

The bright sunshine only lasted until late afternoon. Gradually the familiar purple-black clouds started gathering away toward the west, with curling thunder-tops that fell in on themselves. The wind rose and the temperature started its downward slide.

"Snow," said Lee.

"Yeah," replied Dave. "Find some place for us to camp before it hits. That valley ahead looks a possible."

They'd been moving for about four hours, covering close on twelve miles. Dave figured that they should be able to hit around twenty-five miles a day, more if they found a safe highway. That would bring them back to Cody Heights in a month. Say by the middle of August.

"Home." He tried the word, finding it lay flat and strange on his tongue. There was no way of knowing if "home" was still there. Odd snips of news, mostly near the beginning, had mentioned California slipping inexorably into the Pacific. The San Andreas and Hayward sliding several miles all at once, snuffing out the entire San Francisco and Oakland conurbation. Others talked about a monstrous tidal wave that had crushed Los Angeles and brought the sea into the foothills of the Sierras.

But nobody really knew anything. There was news up to the last hour of the last day. Then, moments later, it was the first hour of the first day. And everything was plain gone.

"Think that yellow-haired guy'll make it, Dad?" asked Lee. "I heard him yelling after us for hours." He paused. "Well...at least a half hour."

Dave stopped breaking trail, closing his eyes and taking several slow, deep breaths, watching them plume out in front of him in the chilly air. The forest around them was totally silent.

"You did well, Lee. Really. I never thought when we first...well, you know all 'bout that. You've seen it, same as me. But we talked about it. How folks here and there might get driven mad. That's why we broke into the gun store and got what we got."

The boy grinned, wiping brittle ice from around the hood of the parka. "Sure. Your face when that door opened and that old guy stood there. 'I'm sorry to trouble, sir, but we need these weapons. I'll pay with my Am-Ex, of course.' Your face when he said, 'I don't give a flying fuck what you want. I come to steal some shotgun shells meself.' And you a member of the Chamber of Commerce, Dad.''

Dave Rand grinned back. "I thought that was a bad moment. Didn't know they got worse." He tried to keep himself shaved, but it was difficult, and now he had crystals of glittering ice gathering in the stubble along his jawline.

"Think he'll make it?"

Dave knew who he meant. "Probably not, son. Melmoth here did a good job on his face. Lost some blood and he was in shock. On his own up there. Shit, how do I know?''

The dog had heard his name spoken and pushed his flank against Dave's leg, looking up at him. There was dark blood matted along his muzzle, and Dave thought he'd have to try and clean it off when they camped for the night. The first few flakes of snow came biting in on a cold blue norther, and he shivered.

"Let's get on, Lee."

THE BUILDING must have been built as a refuge for hikers. It had sturdy walls of cemented stone and a beamed roof. A large open fireplace was half-filled with pale gray ash. A single table with a broken leg was the only furniture. The shutters over one of the windows had been torn off, probably for firewood, and several panes of glass were broken. Layers of dark green material had been hammered over the holes, making the place reasonably weatherproof.

"Looks good." Dave eased the heavy pack off his shoulders and laid it carefully on the dirt floor of the hut. It would make a pleasant change not to have to raise the tent in a howling blizzard and try and secure the flimsy guylines. For once they could sleep easy and safe. Nobody was going to be around in this kind of whiteout. Looking around, it didn't look as if anyone had been there for eighteen months or more.

"Shall I bring in some kindling?"

"Yeah. Don't go more'n thirty paces from the hut and keep your direction clear in your head."

Lee laughed. "One day you'll trust me, Dad."

"That'll be the day, pilgrim," said Dave, deepening his voice to imitate John Wayne. The cowboy had been dead for about seventy years, but his vids were still shown.

Lee didn't respond, stooping to pat the dog and then huddling into the collar of his parka and pushing his way out into the whirling blizzard. Dave started to unpack the sleeping bags, laying them side by side in front of what might hopefully become a fire. It would be a rare luxury for them. Kneeling on the packed earth, he tried to remember how many times they'd enjoyed real warmth. It wasn't more than a dozen times in the past year and a half, and it was now becoming difficult to remember what summer was *really* like. Hot sun and clear skies of blue. Since the Hit, it had been almost nothing but semidarkness at the break of noon and a descent into permanent chill. Those golden days were beginning to seem like a dream, a myth.

At the beginning people had said that it would only last a few days. Then it became weeks, and now, months.

Dave Rand didn't know what people, those who survived, were saying now. He and Lee had kept to themselves for long months.

The supplies of dried and vac-sealed food were running low again. It was one of the big worries. At the beginning it had been easy to find places to raid, like the weapons store. But as time crept by, those places would become fewer. And that meant falling back totally on survival skills.

Out of the wind, the hut already seemed warm, though he could see his breath frosting the still air. As Dave took off his own insulated jacket, his hand encountered his wallet, zipped into an inside pocket.

Some paper money, fives and a couple of tens. Kept for nostalgia. Or, he thought ruefully, to light a fire some time. As the government collapsed, so the entire financial structure of the United States crumbled with it. Barter was the new way of transaction, barter or simple theft.

His Am-Ex card had come in useful three or four times. It was great for forcing locks open.

There was an array of credit and membership cards, each one in its own little plastic envelope. Dave flicked through them, his eye caught by a brown card. National Trust, it said. Family membership for the Rands for 2048. That had been the year of their trip to England. It figured that England's green and pleasant land with its honey colored manor and twisting, hedge-lined lanes must have gone the same way as America.

The last thing Dave looked at was the family photograph.

A laser-pic of the five of them together, only days before the endless winter began.

The little comp-gas lamp he'd put on the table was flickering uneasily. They'd got two replacement cylinders for it, but they only lasted around thirty hours each. Soon they'd be looking at some gloomy nights. Dark on dark.

They'd been standing out on their patio, with the edge of the pool just visible in the far left corner. Melmoth hadn't been keen on posing and was a blurred shape escaping to the right.

Dave had set the camera and had joined the others, kneeling in the foreground. He wore his Forty-Niners sweatshirt and pale blue chinos. Janine was at the centre, her arms around her daughters, with Lee a little off to the side. She was wearing a patterned paisley top and shorts. Her long black hair was tied back, and sunglasses hid her eyes. She had what Dave called her "semi-secret smile" on.

Ellie was fourteen or fifteen. A trim copy of her mother with same raven hair and brown eyes. Standing with her arms folded protectively across her chest, embarrassed by her skimpy new bikini. Roxanne would have been just eight. Favoring Dave's slightly lighter coloring, with piercing green eyes. The sun had caught her in a rare smile, reflecting off the silver braces that were the reason for the rarity of the grin. She stood looking boldly at the camera, in jeans and a T-shirt proclaiming her latest favorite pop group: Potted Peaces.

Lee was a year younger than Ellie. Which meant, Dave worked out, that the girl must have been fifteen at the time. Because he remembered that Lee's fourteenth birthday had taken place only days before. The boy had shot up in height that year, topping six feet, and the basketball and hoop had been an inevitable gift.

Shortly after that, Janine had taken Ellie and Roxanne on a vacation to Memphis, birthplace of her mother. And he'd gone off for a brief few days backpacking with Lee. In the past four or five years, he and Janine had often taken breaks apart. Both of them were aware that this was one of the symptoms that all was no longer totally well with their relationship. But it wasn't something that either of them talked about.

That particular road of thought was one that Dave Rand had traveled very frequently in the first months after the Hit. Now it came less often. But the pain was still startlingly fresh.

There was the sound of someone pounding on the heavy door, and he went quickly to heave it open, letting in a flurry of snow that surrounded the whited figure of his son. He was carrying an armful of dried wood.

"DAD?"

Dave looked up, seeing his son's face glowing in the light of the crackling fire and recognizing that there was something there of himself. The long jaw and the deep-set eyes. It was an odd feeling, like when he used to shave every morning and sometimes glimpsed his own father peering back at him from the steam-misted surface.

"You said, first off, that there wasn't any point going home."

The small dish of veg-sub curry was almost finished. Dave always tried to relish every slow mouthful, believing it made him feel more full. He dug at it with the broad blade of his pocketknife, then licked the steel clean.

"Yeah. That's right, Lee. I did. During those first days . . . all fire and shock and blackness . . . from what we heard before we took to the back-country . . . it sounded like there was no hope at all for Mom and the girls."

"I know that. Man said the epicenter was somewheres in Virginia, didn't he? Said there wasn't a soul alive for five hundred miles around. Said the cities were all wiped out. And that meant Memphis would have missed the last chopper out."

Dave carefully wiped the knife dry on his pants. "I don't think . . ." He tried to pick his words with great care. "I don't think, son, that there's any hope for them. But if... if by some luck or other they got clear, then they might head for Cody Heights. See?"

"Sure." There was a world of mingled hope and disbelief in that single syllable. "Guess I'll turn in, Dad."

Outside, the wind had dropped from its banshee wail to a steady pounding. Seeking out the tiny cracks in the walls, bringing in whispers of snow crystals that piled in corners. The fire was sinking, and Dave reached out and put on another couple of branches. It flared up, throwing a series of dancing shadows on the plastered ceiling.

He rolled himself in the sleeping bag, looking across at his son. The boy had tucked his scattergun near his head, as Dave had taught him. There was no lock on the door, and Dave had the Czech Skorpion Mk3 machine pistol ready by his hand. Not that anybody, or anything, was likely to be out and about in a storm of such ferocity.

"If it eases, we'll make a good start tomorrow morning, Lee. Sleep well."

"Thanks, Dad. Be good to be home. You really do want to go there, Dad?"

Dave Rand hesitated. "Guess I do. We got to go somewhere, son."

"Right. Goodnight."

"Goodnight."

Then it was only the crackling of the fire and the night-long moans of the storm around them.

By morning the blizzard had moved on eastward, away from them.

5

From the 14 November 2048 edition of the Leonie Lesser syndicated chat show, "Lesser Is More." The guest in this segment was a popular English astronomer, Mortimer Smith.

L.L. What about all this talk of heavenly bodies, Professor?

M.S. Pure speculation at present, my dear. Nobody can predict an eccentric performer like our asteroid friend.

L.L. You should watch the Giants if you wanna see eccentric performers, Doc.

M.S. But there is a serious side to all this. Adastreia, as the little rogue is called, could do terrible harm *if* it ever did come our way. It's about fifteen miles across and could impact our planet at a speed in excess of eighty thousand miles per hour as well as—

L.L. Come on, cut down on the figures, will you! You'll be describing how to play cricket next... All we want to know is will it hit or will it won't hit us?

M.S. Well, I certainly don't think it will, but then again, there's not a true . . .

L.L. Tell you what, Prof., if it does hit us, then you can come and kiss my asteroid!

Later that same evening the production team of "Lesser is More" receive a confidential call from a Government Broadcasting Control Authority spokesperson about one of the items on their show.

6

Dave Rand steadied the lightweight **N**ikon 9x35 binoculars and scanned the valley floor ahead of them, moving the glasses slowly from left to right. He paused to check there was no possibility of the watery sunlight reflecting off the coated lenses.

"Anything?" whispered Lee, lying prone beside him on the crown of the ridge.

"No. Thought I saw someone moving in the shadows by that gas station. But if there was someone, they're gone now."

They'd been hiking for eight days, most times exceeding Dave's expectation of how far they might cover in a single dawn-to-dusk.

It was a little after sunup, the night's frost still leaving a biting chill in the air. An hour or so after dusk Dave had heard what sounded like a car engine, somewhere toward the township, but it faded away and blurred into a dream. When he woke, he wasn't even sure that he'd heard the sound at all.

Food was low, and it was becoming essential that they find something in the next day. They'd reached old 260, cutting north and west off U.S. Highway 60 just past Show Low. Dave's rough plan was to follow it to Payson, looping around Prescott, hoping to avoid the huge conurbation of Phoenix. The bigger the city, the better the reason for giving it a wide berth.

"That a death pit?" asked Lee, pointing with a gloved forefinger to a pair of trenches that ran along the back of a single-story shopping mart. One of them began at the fence of the church-yard.

"Could be." Focusing the glasses, he brought the place into sharp relief. "Can't tell at this distance," he said.

Every community seemed to have death pits. Since they'd been careful to keep well away from large communities, Dave couldn't even begin to imagine how they'd coped with their dead.

News, once the winters had begun to bite, was necessarily vague and confused, coming from a whole variety of unreliable sources. But there was a general pattern that Dave Rand had to regard as being close to the truth.

Some people had made an effort to stock up on food and clean water, but a whole lot more hadn't bothered, contenting themselves with the comfortable belief that it wouldn't ever happen.

When it did, life came to a grinding halt. Food shops were emptied in the first two or three days, except in some places where there had been mass evacuations. Factories all closed as the power stopped.

Water supplies dried up as pumping and purifying stations ceased. The first deaths in cities were probably from thirst, not counting the huge spate of suicides. After thirst came hunger, and on its heels rode the grinning specter of starvation. As an accountant Dave was interested in figures, but he knew that nobody would ever be able to calculate how many died or how long it took them. His own guesstimate was that relatively few went in the first week or so. Then, in cities the trickle became a torrent. There simply wasn't *any* food and no way of getting any. His mind veered away from trying to think of how it had been.

What he knew, actually *knew*, was that every single settlement they'd risked visiting for supplies had its own death pit.

"Split up?"

Dave took a slow, deep breath as he looked along the deserted main street of Caleton, population 8476. Tumbleweed blew along the dusty street, swept clear of snow by a biting westerly. The weather had been a little warmer for a couple of days, but the roofs still held pockets of white, cradled in the shadows around dormers and attics.

"We'll take a chance. But we keep tight, Lee. You to the left side and I'll take the right. And watch out for the upper windows and the alleys. Gun loaded? Good. Slow and careful."

It didn't look too promising for food. But it was worth just checking through, then taking a look at some of the outlying houses. Experience had already taught the father-and-son team that the more isolated homes were more likely to be untouched.

One of the first houses they came to had a large mural painted on its end wall, faded and scoured by sun and wind and sand.

It showed a group of young people of different races working together on what looked like a barn raising. Everyone seemed to be absurdly happy, grinning fit to bust. It was no surprise to find that the building had once housed an Episcopalian mission. Dave noticed that someone had worked on it with graffiti, presumably in the last days of the old world. A crude ball of orange fire, vaguely reminiscent of the Japanese flag, was painted in the sky, along with the words, in the same virulent color: Please, What We Deserve, Please, Please . . .

There were surprisingly few signs of any looting in Caleton. A couple of stores had their windows smashed in, and two or three more had obvious damage to the locks on their front doors.

As in other places they'd risked entering, it was the same kind of stores that had been hit. Food and liquor first. Then the gun store and sporting goods emporium. And oddly, what with the power gone, people also went for vids and laser players.

Thoreau's Books wasn't touched.

Dave Rand looked in the dusty glass, eyeing the piles of '48's bestsellers and walking guides to Arizona backcountry, wondering if it was worth packing some. But there was always scrap paper and bark to help light a fire. Books weren't worth the trouble to carry.

A dry-goods store had a large white notice, finger-painted on the inside of its windows. Pre-Comet Specials . . . 40% Off All Marked Lines!

A torn edge of a curtain fluttered from a broken window of the Caleton Imperial Hotel. It caught Dave's eye, and he swung the muzzle of his Browning 245 12-gauge to cover it, grinning self-consciously at his reaction.

"What's that place alongside you with the broken glass?" he shouted.

Lee smiled at him, teeth showing white in the shadow of the overhanging second story. "Porn-book shop, Dad." Peering at a sign that dangled from a broken chain, he laughed.

"What's the joke?" Turning his head on one side, Dave could also manage to read the sign. The shop had been called Jerkov's.

"You get it, Dad? It means . . ."

"Yeah, Lee. I do know what it means. Thanks."

His nostrils suddenly caught the lost scent of roasting meat. Rich and tempting, like a friend's barbecue on a Pleasant Valley Sunday back home. Without even being aware of it, the man began to salivate at the smell.

On the far side, Lee paused, looking over toward his father, his head on one side as he tried to work out where the scent was coming from. Dave had already learned to trust Lee's sense of smell. He'd smoked for most of his adult life, finally giving it up on his thirtieth birthday. But Lee had never smoked, not even an occasional joint with school friends. In the past eighteen months, he'd frequently caught the odor of a wood fire long before Dave had picked it up.

"Where?" called Dave.

"That way." Lee pointed to the left, in the general direction of the whitewashed church spire that dominated Caleton.

THE TRENCHES behind the shopping mart were what they'd suspected. One of them had been neatly excavated and as neatly filled in. The other one was ragged and crooked, only filled in for part of its hundred-foot length.

Dave was leading the way, picking carefully across rough ground lightly covered in snow. One of the things that he'd become far more conscious of since the endless dusks began was the risk of survival living. No doctors around, and Blue Cross worth less than a packet of freeze-dried soup. A sprained ankle could bring a serious hazard of death.

"Can I check 'em out, Dad?"

"I'll come with you."

It was odd. The back of the main street looked exactly like the back of any small town, and there was no sense at all of the monstrous scale of the world disaster. The buildings were more or less the same—maybe a little dirtier than in old times. There were three rusting, burned-out trucks behind a drugstore. The church was ahead of them, a thin column of smoke roiling into the sky from behind it. There was still no sign of life.

They crossed the frozen, rutted ground of the first of the pits. At one end there was a wooden sign, split in half. It was badly weathered but it appeared, from a distance, to be a long, long list of names.

The second, unfinished grave didn't have even the remains of a sign on it.

Lee reached the gaping, open end of the pit a few paces ahead of his father. He stopped and looked in then turned away, his face working with emotion, eyes searching beyond Dave. He turned back again for confirmation of his disbelief.

Dave joined him, letting his hand rest gently on the boy's shoulder.

The first impression reminded him of some ancient vid he'd watched, huddled on the long sofa in their home, with his arm around Janine and a three-parts-empty jug of brew on the glass-topped table. Back when they used to put their arms around each other a lot.

The vid had been set in Cambodia, or some place out East. Maybe about the Viet War. And a guy had stumbled into a muddy pit filled with decaying corpses that had been executed by suffocation with blue plastic bags. A bright blue plastic.

Here the bags were a sort of olive green color. But there was the same jumble that filled the eyes with a tangled horror.

None of the neatness and order of a civic funeral parlor. No flowers and memorial tablets of sun-bleached stone and italic, sharply-incised script for the names and the dates.

The constant cold weather had preserved many of the bodies that had spilled from the bags or been torn by the razored beaks of crows or the worrying teeth of the hunting packs of coyotes. They lay in the deep pit of raw earth like surreal furniture that had tumbled from the back of an overturned truck.

Mostly it was bones amid the sea of flapping green plastic, like shrouding seaweed enveloping the bodies of drowned seamen. White bones, with shreds of leathery skin hanging from them. Arms wrenched away from shoulders, and skulls that snarled up at the leaden sky.

"Jesus, Dad... It's like there isn't any dignity left."

There was nothing else to say, and they averted their eyes.

As they walked on toward the church, there was a faint tremor of the earth. Just enough to rattle a metal sign away to their right. In the past eighteen

months minor quakes had become such an every-
day fact of life that neither of them made any
comment on it.

"Quiet and careful," whispered Dave. He and
Lee had taken off their heavy packs, caching them
in the porch of the church.

Repent and Even Now Ye Shall Be Spared, said
the quote, attributed to someone called the archi-
mandrite of New Jerusalem.

The smell of cooking meat was overpowering,
and came from a fire that smoked and flared just
the other side of the wooden building. They were
now close enough to catch the low murmur of
conversation. Dave had considered trying a
friendly, open approach, reasoning that there
might still be some ordinary, decent folks left in
the state.

In the end he decided to step softly and carry the
scatterguns, charged and ready.

"Ready?"

"Yeah." Lee licked his lips nervously, breathing fast and light.

They stepped around the corner, to confront a
truly weird scene.

A big fire was melting away the snow for thirty
yards around, with a tripod of metal erected over
it. From a large rusting hook hung a battered iron

cauldron, black with soot. Dave and Lee were close enough to be able to see a rich, dark liquid bubbling in the pot.

"We'd like..." Dave began, addressing the half-dozen figures huddled around the fire. But that was as far as he got.

7

TOP SECRET. Totality Security Memo, Clearance Levels 17 and above ONLY. From Def-Ast to Chiefs Allsec. 15 November 2048.

Deep space surveillance revealed the threat potential of Adastreia going rogue as early as October. Usual precautions were taken to control information. However, a local paper in Colorado—see earlier memo on *Drowned Creek Picayune and Weekly Advertiser*—leaked the story in a premature manner. Follow-ups in press and on a syndicated talk show—later contacted but not at sufficient speed—have meant undesirable publicity about the threat.

Our people believe the risk to Earth is significant but negligible. Comp-preds show prob-factors of less than 17% of severe impact. Megacull potential is less than 6.85%.

Adastreia is in an eccentric and unpredictable orbit, heading toward this sector of space.

Note that only low-level contact on this subject has so far been detailed with "Others." Level 4 contact is advised with powers designated friendly, and Level 3 for all others.

The official line for the President will be formulated within the next six working days and will be adhered to by all advisers at all times. The media people in our direct sphere can expect to be informed of where their duty lies.

ComSecProp will meet daily and consult with Def-Ast on any change in threat status of Adastreia. All negative reports must—*repeat, must*—be suppressed to prevent any concern on the part of the people.

We are informed that there won't be a significant temporal delay before the threat becomes easily visible through normally obtained optical devices.

ENDS.

8

The six crouching figures jerked around as though impelled by a single chain, staring at the two armed interlopers. They screamed in shock and anger, almost simultaneously drawing long-bladed butcher's knives from under their heavy cloaks of matching dark blue, decorated with dozens of white crosses. Their faces were concealed by white ski masks, with a single crimson cross embroidered at the center of the forehead.

Dave didn't hesitate. He pulled on the trigger of the shotgun, aiming at the ground halfway between himself and the group. The shot dug out a spatter of gravel, making the six halt in their tracks.

"Get the fuck away!" he yelled, waving the Browning to back up the threat.

"Yeah, or you're all dead!" added Lee, voice thin and high with the tension of the moment.

"The food's ours," yelled the shortest of the six in a deep, throaty voice. "You leave us be, or else."

"Or else what? We got the guns. You move on. We won't take it all."

"You dirty lying shitters!" yelped another of the hooded gang.

It was almost a replay of the attack in the forest. But this time Dave was fully in control. He waved the gun a second time. "Next shot'll blow someone's legs off," he warned. "I said we'd only take some of the meat. We'll leave the rest and move on."

"You mean it?"

"I don't tell lies, mister. You all go slow and easy and leave me and the boy to it. Don't try anything on, and nobody'll get themselves hurt. Just go."

Reluctantly, their knives still unsheathed, the six backed away, eyes glittering behind the masks. Dave and Lee watched them go, keeping the guns up until the group had vanished across the far side of the empty lot.

"Think they'll try anything?"

"Hope not. Plenty of daylight left. We've got all the firepower we need. Just keep a good look out for them, Lee."

For the first time they could savor the smell of the meat and relish the thought of a good, belly-filling meal. There were hunks of fresh-baked sourdough bread, and a glass pitcher of powdered milk. The men had left behind their tin plates, spoons and mugs.

They sat down on either side of the bright fire so that they could cover both fields of view. Lee had a view of the nineteenth-century church and his father was able to watch out across the open lot facing a street of low houses, each one surrounded by a frost-dead hedge.

Dave handed the boy a plate and a spoon. "Break off a chunk of bread for yourself, son. Use it to mop up the good gravy."

The cauldron also held some vegetables, floating in the lightly scummy water. Carrots and some turnip greens, with a smattering of black-eyed peas. The meat was in sizable pieces, and Dave stirred it around with his spoon, fetching up a couple of glistening bones.

"Hell, this surely smells good," he said. "Want me to serve you?"

"Please, Dad," Lee said, holding his plate out. Dave ladled in a generous helping, making sure his son had some of the more succulent hunks of meat.

"Smells real critical." Lee wiped the back of his hand across his mouth and watched as his father served himself a brimming bowl. "What kind of meat is it, Dad?" he asked.

"Beef?"

The boy fished out a piece and held it on his spoon, examining it. "Could be pork, I think. Yeah, it looks more like pork."

"Right. I don't care if it's whale or horse or any damned creature."

"Must be more in that bucket there. Maybe we could take that with us."

Dave glanced down, seeing a galvanized bucket, its lid stuck crookedly on the top. Across from him, Lee was still holding his first spoonful to his nose, inhaling, eyes closed, a beatific smile on his lips. Dave took the lid off and looked inside.

"Oh, fuck! Oh, no, fuck! Lee....Noooo!"

The meat wasn't difficult to identify; the human femur is not like the bone from any edible animal. And Dave could see that one of the hands still had a cheap silver ring on its third finger. The eyes might have been plucked from the small skull, but the long strands of blond hair still remained, pasted to the peeled bone.

Almost retching, Dave replaced the lid on the cauldron and motioned for Lee to follow him as he moved out. Neither of them spoke for a long time, overcome as they were by what they had just witnessed.

They struggled on westward, scavenging and hunting where they could. Dave pointed out several times that in some ways they were lucky about the weather. With the overcast skies and the biting cold, it meant they had to keep moving to stay warm.

"Normal summer on this highway, and you'd be lucky to make ten miles on foot. And you'd have to carry at least a gallon of water each. Noon temperatures would've been way, way over the hundred. Out in the sun it'd be around one-fifty. Hot enough—"

"To fry an egg on the hood of a car. Yeah, Dad. You've told me."

They kept a good schedule, following the main routes where it seemed safe. Only four times in four weeks did they see any vehicles not counting a half-dozen ox- and horse-drawn carts. There were two trucks, with armed men riding shotgun on them, and a couple of private automobiles. Both of them were towing a trailer that Dave guessed must hold some hoarded gas supplies. A shot was fired at them from the second car, a flame red sedan, but it went way wide. They didn't bother to shoot back.

Crossing what had been the desert was the most dangerous, and Dave decided to make a travois, Indian-style, to drag along the carcass of a large buck deer he'd managed to bring down with the SIG-Sauer 941 bolt-action rifle.

One night they were camping close by the old Twentynine Palms reservation. It was a clear night with a harsh frost, and their fire of bleached kindling was burning too fast to last them through the hours of darkness. But it was a cheerful blaze, and Dave allowed it full rein.

"Think the weather'll ever get warmer?" asked Lee, lying back, tucked into his sleeping bag. They never bothered erecting the tent if the nights stayed dry.

"Who knows? Some of the gloomiest predictions talked about a nuke winter that would last forever, kill all the crops and trees, animals and people. It hasn't been that bad—not after the first big strike. I kind of feel it's not so cold this year as it was last. Bit more sun. Maybe the few of us left might have a decent future. One day."

"Dad?"

"What?" Leaning back on one elbow, Dave stared into the brightness of the fire.

"Don't sked off or anything. Just keep kind of quiet."

His son's hi-board slang was a constant source of amusement to Dave Rand. He and Janine had often teased the boy about it. But since the Big Hit, Lee hadn't used it so much.

"I won't 'sked' off. What's the matter?"

"Company, Dad, but don't rush."

Dave felt the sudden cold at the pit of his stomach. As far as he knew, they were long miles from another human being. If they were caught like this . . .

He managed to keep his voice as calm as his son's. "See how many?"

"Dozen or so. Horses. Looks like they're maybe Indians, Dad. They're behind you and just sort of sitting there an' watching us."

"Guns?"

"They're on the edge of the light from the fire. Think so. I can make out reflections off metal. Try turning around real slow, Dad."

Dave eased his head to the side, using his peripheral vision to pick up their visitors. Indians, probably Navaho. Or they might even be Apache. Chiricahua? Short and stocky men with hair tied back in bandannas, looking like refugees from any of a thousand Western vids.

He turned a little more until he faced them. They were riding sturdy ponies, and they were armed.

"There's a shallow creek bed about a hundred yards behind you, Lee," he said, trying to avoid moving his lips. "Shooting starts, grab your rifle and the SIG-Sauer and go for it."

Lee didn't reply. The nearest of the Indians heeled his mount in the ribs, walking it a few steps forward. He was an old man with fine silver hair and a weathered face. He pointed at Dave with the muzzle of an ancient M-16 carbine.

"Your son?"

"Yes."

"You are alone?"

"Yes."

"You have come far?"

"Over in New Mexico. We're heading back to our home in California."

One of the other Indians said something, bringing a burst of guttural laughter. But the old man didn't even smile.

"There is no more California. The sea has risen and swallowed it. As the fires and the breathing of the earth have darkened the sky and the land. It has all gone. And we remain. We, the people, remain here in our land."

Dave nodded. "I heard something of that. But we have to try."

The Indian sat motionless. Moments passed in stillness. Far off to the east there was a thunderstorm raging, lacing the sky with darts of silver, but so far away that it was soundless.

"You have food?"

Since the half-eaten body of the deer was in clear sight, there wasn't much point in lying. Dave nodded. "Yeah. We got food."

"Water?"

"Some. Enough, I think."

"That's good." The deep-set eyes bored into David Rand's face. "There has been so much death that the land calls out for relief."

"That's true. Thanks for your concern for me and the boy."

The Indian nodded, firelight dancing off the silver decorations around his belt and across the chest of his fringed jacket. He lifted his hand and then wheeled his pony around, leading the band off, the darkness swallowing them into itself.

"So long," called Lee.

That encounter at last left Dave feeling a glimmer of hope for life, for humanity itself.

But the nearer they got to home, the more his depression deepened. Though they were irreparably altered, they passed more and more places that rang bells in his memory. Times past, with Janine and their growing trio of little ones. The good, warm times that would never vanish from his memory, overshadowing the more recent distance and bickering.

He'd once copied out a few lines from a poem, though he couldn't recall where it came from. As they trudged into California and toward the snow-blanketed Sierras, Dave found himself repeating the lines like a mantra to steer them into harbor.

> I miss her at the turning of the tide,
> I miss her in the weeping of the rain,
> and last year's loving, bitter, still remains.

It was the middle of the morning of 17 August when Dave and Lee Rand finally reached Cody Heights and their home.

9

18 November 2048. Translation from article in Zvezda, *17 November 2048.*

Introduction: This publication, whose name simply means "Star," is a small-circulation Russian magazine that is only released to State-approved astronomers and space experts. It is not available to any member of the general Russian public.

This is a synopsized translation of the main body of the article and must only be released to anyone with Sec-Clearance of 17 and above.

The outer-space probe base centered at Ozhbarchik on the Kamchatka Peninsula has been tracking the breakaway—literally, "free-moving"—asteroid, called Adastreia, for several days. It is believed that its path is also being followed by astronomers and observatories in the United States, Southern Africa,

India, China, Australia, the United Kingdom and several countries in Europe and South America. But note that no public announcement has yet been made in a single one of these countries.

The movement of the body is exceedingly eccentric, and there is a substantial proportion of belief that suspects it may eventually break up and thus present even more problems. But possibly none of them will strike Earth.

An American document shows they have a comp-pred of 6.85% on megacull potential. Our own estimates are in this region but a little higher. Final figures are not yet available for release.

In the event of Adastreia becoming closer and more visible, instructions should be swiftly given to all regional committees and military commanders with a suggested course of action.

This should particularly involve the positive disencouragement of population movements away from centers of communication.

Further information can be obtained within normal hours from unlisted number 24/9/42/JWL.

P.S. Note there are uncorroborated reports from agencies that publication of *Zvezda* has been temporarily suspended

10

The seventeenth day of August in 2050 had
dawned with a steady drizzle coming in off the
Pacific—an ocean that was now over a hundred
miles farther east than it had been a year and a
half earlier. The surf that had previously lapped
the shores close to Santa Barbara, Morro Bay and
San Simeon now crashed against the foothills of
the Greenhorns and the Tehachapi Mountains.

If Dave Rand had wanted to drive to the sea
from his house in Cody Heights, it would now
only take him about fifteen minutes.

But the road leading to Bakersfield had totally
disappeared beneath billions of tons of shifted
earth and rock. There was still a looping trail in
the direction of his house from the south and east,
but even that was badly damaged by the unthink-
able quakes that followed the Big Hit.

It was that same seismic damage that had preserved the house, isolated on a spur of rock above
a hanging valley, from being ravaged by looters.
Nobody had bothered to try and get through to the

building, perched invisibly behind a screen of ponderosa pine and redwood.

Dave had bought the property from a bankrupt installer of satellite inter-vid dishes in 2042, moving with his young family from their previous home in a shady side street of Encino. The property market had been depressed by one of the periodic scares about gas supplies from the Middle East, and most people were frightened off by the place's isolation.

It was a mainly single-story house with one bedroom on the second floor. The shingled roof sloped steeply to accommodate the normally heavy winter snowfalls in that part of the mountains. There was a basic plot of around two and a half acres of scrubby garden and a smallish pool. A chain-link fence demarcated a steep drop to a ravine at the rear of the property.

A big spacious living area was open to the five bedrooms and a couple of bathrooms, with the big eat-in kitchen protruding from the rear. A double garage at the side of the building normally held their two vehicles, as well as the usual assortment of bikes, old and new, tools, and eighteen years of household rubbish.

They had mains electricity, as well as a miniature generator for emergencies. The windows were all double glazed, and solar panels were set in the roof.

Dave stood close by his son in the bitter cold of their living room, looking out through the dirty, rain-smeared windows into the misty valley below them. He experienced a sense of disbelief at being back at a place where their life had had a normal flow. The nightmare changes and this reminder of peace, normalcy, clashed in his mind and threatened to bring tears to his eyes. Memories flooded back to him of so many good times, and some more recent times that had been less good. Despite the problems that had arisen between Janine and himself, he would still have given anything to have her and the girls back with him at that moment.

"Want me to go try get the generator running?" asked Lee, making him start.

"Yes, of course. Take the shotgun with you. Doesn't look like anyone's been around, but..."

Lee patted him patronizingly on the shoulder. "Sure, Dad. I know how it is for you old farts. Gotta be careful, right?"

"Right." He grinned. Watching his son go out of the front door, passing in front of the picture windows. In the past day or so, the boy had been visibly happier, making the familiar jokes, eager to get home.

There had been the single moment, as they came up the driveway when he'd almost expected to find everybody at home, and he felt a wave of disappointment at the realization that Janine, Ellie and Roxanne really weren't there. They both knew that all three were dead, had to be dead.

Outside he could hear the splutter of the gas engine being hand pulled. It had always been a stubborn machine to start.

Dave couldn't recall how much gas they had left. There was a hundred-gallon tank, and he thought that it had been fairly full when they left.

"Hot bath," he whispered. "My God, a real hot bath."

In the end he let Lee take the first dip in the steaming tub, and he went about, taking stock of what had to be done.

Janine had always kept the larder shelves well stocked, and there were dozens and dozens of tins and packets of food. When the power had failed, the freezer went with it. Fortunately the cold weather meant that the rotted contents weren't too disgusting. While his son languished in his bath with some of his favorite Tex-Mex blues music blaring through the house, Dave emptied out the

freezer and gave the whole place a superficial ti-
dying.

He found himself constantly stumbling over the
memories.

Ellie's room, the walls lined with 3-D las-posters
of her best-loved stars and singers. In Roxanne's
small side room where was Mr. Boffo, the soft doll
with the blue nose, lying tucked into her bed, as if
he were waiting for the little girl to return.

Dave leaned over and patted the creature on the
head, feeling his own tears brimming in his eyes.

The bedroom he'd shared with Janine was
slowly warming up as the power brought heat to
the radiators. He and Lee had agreed that they
wouldn't risk lighting the fire that was already laid
in the hearth. As long as they kept the drapes shut,
it was unlikely that anyone would notice that the
house was occupied. But a column of smoke
would bring any scavenger from miles about.

Dave sat on the bed, letting his eyes catalog the
familiar room.

Family pix on the table beside the bed, every
one with its own poignant moment, frozen forever like an iridescent beetle trapped in amber.

He opened his wardrobe, looking at the row of
suits that hung there like replicates of his own
past, each one eager to bear him into Bakersfield

and into his office. Neat loafers, their sheen dulled by eighteen months of neglect. The only section that interested him was the drawers of thick sweaters and his socks-and-underclothes shelf.

As he turned around, his eye was caught by something under the bed. Resting his hand on the duvet, he stopped and plucked it up. He fingered the fragile silk, red as arterial blood, fringed with pale cream lace. The temptation to press it to his face and try to catch the ghost of her body was almost overwhelming. But Dave heard the sound of water draining away and the bathroom door clicking open. He quickly stuffed the panties into his pocket and stood up, smoothing down the bedspread.

LEE WAS HOLDING the phone in his hand when Dave finally finished his own bath. The water had been wonderful, scented with pine oil, easing away the accumulated dirt and stiffness and bringing back to him the almost-forgotten vestiges of comfort.

"Anyone there, son?" he asked jokingly, then suddenly realized that the boy was weeping. Great gobbets of tears coursed over the fresh-shaved cheeks to drop onto the shoulders of his terry-cloth robe. His shoulders were shaking with the violence of his emotion.

"It's dead. Not crackling or static or anything. Quiet as a . . . as a grave, Dad."

Dave moved to his side, hugging him tightly, holding him against the shuddering force of his grief. "It's okay, Lee. Course it is. We know the score. It's not the bottom of the ninth. More like the top of the first, for us."

"Mom and Roxie and Ellie . . ." The boy's sobbing nearly choked him, and he fought for breath. "I can't believe we'll never . . . you know, see them again. There's not even any place for us to visit them, like with Grandad and Grandma. It's not fair, Dad. I'm sorry . . . but it's not."

THE RAIN STOPPED during the afternoon, and Dave walked through the garden, saddened at the desolation wrought by the long winter. This time of year it would have been ablaze with color, the borders neat and trim. Melmoth wandered at his heels, sniffing around him as if he knew that the place had become a strange mix of the familiar and the odd.

The pool had particularly bewildered the stocky pit bull. It had been drained when the family went their separate ways, but the deep frost must have probed at a weakness and burst a main valve. It was now filled brim-high with a solid block of gray-blue ice, holding pockets of rain in the scoured hollows.

Melmoth had snarled at the frozen pool, the sound rumbling deep in his chest. He set a cautious paw on the surface, then another. Finally he risked all four feet, head cocked on one side, eyes narrowed as he looked to Dave for reassurance.

"World's turned upside down, boy," said Dave. "I kind of know how you feel."

Desolately they checked out every nook and cranny by evening, both in the house and the grounds. By evening they were holed up in the living room, surrounded by their own memories.

There was an inch or so remaining in the bottom of the liter of quality brandy they'd brought back from Europe on their long-ago vacation. It was kept for special occasions. Dave held it to the light, looking across the room to where Lee was flicking through some old comics.

"Fancy a drop of armagnac?" he asked.

"What? Me?"

"Sure. It's always been for real special family celebrations. You and me are the family now, Lee. You and me. And we've gotten home. Seems special to me. Want some?"

"Please."

Dave also took the lead crystal tumblers from the shelf, dusting them carefully, wiping them so that every facet shone with a rainbowed brilliance. He poured out the liquor, savoring the way its richness filled the tired air of the house and held out one glass to his son.

He emptied the remaining couple of fingers of armagnac into his own glass and held it out for a toast. The glasses rang with a clear tone.

"To you and me, Lee. To the bad times we've been through and to some better times to come."

"And to the others."

They drank in silence. Soon the bitter, empty feeling crowded around them and they sought refuge in the comforts of bed—a comfort they hadn't enjoyed for a long time. But even that couldn't keep the bad dreams at bay.

They came back, worse than they'd been before. Anxiety nightmares that jerked him awake in a cold sweat, unable for several long seconds to realize where he was. The worst was a recurring one that Dave had suffered from before.

He was in the kitchen at home, though it was slightly different in ways he couldn't understand. He was at the table, his Cheerios in a bowl and a jug of milk at his elbow. Janine was standing by the sink with all three children, doing the dishes.

She was holding a carving knife with a serrated blade, and she kept throwing it in the air and catching it.

When Dave tried to stand up to stop her, he couldn't move from the seat. Janine laughed at him, sending the knife spinning in the air and catching it by the tip between her strong, white teeth. "It's an old Ashanti hunting trick, Dave," she said. "Anyone can do it. Watch the children all have a real good go. You first, Lee."

Dave's fingers curled into claws, drawing blood from his palms, as he struggled to stop the ritual. Fighting for words, helpless, dribbling and drooling soundlessly.

His son took the carving knife from his mother, smiling at his father and making a stage bow. He threw the steel in a shining arc, way high, ten, twenty, fifty feet in the air, through what had been the ceiling of the kitchen.

Dave was up from his chair, but moving with a drugged, hypnotic slowness, watching as the knife began to turn and fall—toward Lee's open mouth.

Dave woke up, the sheets sodden with perspiration, hands sore, tears streaking down his cheeks. Some nights he woke up after the point pierced his son's throat, standing out a clear nine inches behind his neck. On bad nights both the girls also butchered themselves before he managed to struggle free from sleep.

Grateful that he'd awakened before the climax of the nightmare, David eventually drifted off to sleep again. When he finally woke, it was to a sunny dawn, in a warm house, with Lee holding a tray of breakfast for him.

"Orange juice, some kind of dry cereal, condensed milk, canned peaches, powdered-egg omelet and a cup of good strong black coffee."

"Strong enough to float . . ." began Dave, sitting up in bed.

"A horseshoe on," completed the boy. "Sure is. I've fed Melmoth. He looked at the canned meat like it was shit after all that rabbit and deer."

"Where is he?"

"Outside."

Dave nodded, pouring some milk over the cereal, the action bringing back the nightmare. He set that behind him. "Hey, Lee, thanks for this. Nice of you."

"After you've eaten, Dad . . ."

"Yeah?"

"Are we going to talk 'bout what we'll do?"

"Do?" Thoughtfully Dave sipped the coffee. "You mean now we're home you want to hit the road again? Let's rest here a while and kind of charge our batteries. Then think about the first day of the rest of our lives.''

"Sure. But then what?''

Dave pointed at him with a spoon. "Give me a breather, Lee. Haven't had breakfast in bed since last Father's Day...before It hit. But I promise you we'll talk. We can't go on aimlessly, that's for sure.''

Lee paused in the doorway. "Anything else I can get you, Dad?''

"Sure. Some paper and check the mailbox for mail, just in case...''

The moment he'd said that, Dave recognized it was a silly mistake. Mentioning the mailbox would make Lee think of his mother and sisters again, raise his hopes and set him wondering if there might even be a card from them.

"Hey, Dad!'' Lee's face was transfigured. "I'll go check. There might be a letter or...'' His voice faded away as he dashed out of the room and along the corridor.

Dave heard Melmoth's excited barking as the dog followed the boy out of the front door.

Something prompted Dave to lay the tray aside and get out of bed. The water in the heating pipes was murmuring and whistling after the long lay-off. From the window he could see down the driveway to the silver-painted box that said simply: Rand.

Lee was wearing a yellow sweater and white jeans. When he reached the mailbox, he stopped and stood still for several long seconds. Watching him, Dave realized he was holding his breath.

There actually *was* some mail. Lee was holding several envelopes or cards, looking at them and riffling through the pile.

"Oh, Christ!" Dave whispered. His son had just turned and punched the air, jumping high, the pit bull leaping at his heels. Then he began to run toward the house, waving something white in his hand and shouting to his father. All Dave could catch through the double glazing was the single word.

"Alive!"

11

Second draft of President's Address to the Nation. 9pm EST, 25 November 2048.

My fellow Americans,

The time has come to put an ending to the rumors that have been circulating for some days now. There are those among us who erroneously believe that the world is about to end in a cataclysm of fire and megadeath, and these believers have gone about inciting panic with their careless words.

The facts are these. There is an asteroid, called Adastreia, which has come a little loose from its moorings out there in space. It's a little like a pop-up off the bat when nobody quite knows where the ball's going to land.

Is this the end of our world and the American way? Of course it isn't. Even if this bit of cosmic dust happens to blow anywhere near us, we have the technology to blast it clear out of the sky. And if we have to, we will!

But out scientists inform me that the odds of our being hit, even a glancing blow, are about as good as the Padres winning the pennant.

We'll keep you informed through the usual channels, and you can rely on our friends in the media to tell you the truth.

So just carry on with life as usual. This hunk of rock might give us a close shave and a few fireworks, but that's all.

So ease your fears, and let's get back to the business of living. We have a lot of tomorrows.

We are on guard for America, my friends. And a good night to you all.

P.S. Tom—this still needs a hell of a lot of work if we don't want to scare the crap out of people. Let's have another brain-pound at 3 today.

12

The date on the postcard had faded and become almost illegible, but it must have been mailed in January of 2049, only a couple of days before Shocktime.

The Rand mailbox leaked, and the card was warped and slightly dampened. It had also attracted the attention of snails, and one corner had been completely nibbled away.

Dave took it from his son's gloved hand and looked at the picture, taking his time before turning it over to read the message. It was a stereo-tint of a big, flamboyant house called Graceland, which had seemingly been the home of the long-dead rock singer, Elvis Presley, in Memphis, Tennessee.

"Come on, Dad! Read it. Read the card. It's really total!"

"All right, Lee. All right." Turning it over again, Dave found that his fingers were shaking a little.

Perversely he kept himself waiting seconds longer, studying the address, written in Janine's familiar, slanted hand: "Dave & Lee Rand, Overlook, Highridge Canyon Road, Cody Heights, California."

Lee was pleading with him to go on, and he read it out loud. "Hi, guys. Here's the home of the King of R&R. In end big queue so no-show for us. Everyone's full of news of the Big One and where and when it'll hit. Or If. So I called Ma last night, and she said come up see us before B.O. Leaving this a.m. for Montana. Brrr. Girls join in shivery love. See you soon...hopefully. Love, Mom. Watch the skies."

Lee reached out and took the card from him, rereading it himself. "Gee, Dad, they're in Montana. That means they weren't close to Virginia when the Hit came. Montana's a long way off. They could be safe, couldn't they, Dad? Safe?"

Dave nodded, unable to decide what he was feeling. The certainty of the deaths of Janine, Ellie and Roxanne had been a permanent part of his waking days for over eighteen months. Some of the sharp pain had left him, and most of the time now he could think of them without feeling his eyes brim with tears.

Now this.

"They could be. Depends on exactly when they started and how long it took them. The way Janine drives, they'd have done it in a single long day. Yeah, they should have been safe in Montana before the Hit came.''

Lee whooped, dropping to his knees to cuddle the bewildered Melmoth. "Hear that, you ugly bastard? Mom and the girls are alive and well!''

"They were a year and a half ago, son," warned Dave. "So were a lot of people. Now... you've seen it like I have.''

The boy stood up nodding. "Course. Shouldn't have skedded off like that, Dad. But you have to admit...''

Dave smiled. "Yeah. Course I have to admit. It's the most hopeful bit of news we've had in the last eighteen months or so.''

"And we'll go up to Montana? To Granny Bronsky? When?''

"Hold on a minute, Lee. We'll think about this and talk it through this morning. Check out the four-by wag and provisions and maps and all that stuff. We rush off without one in the chamber, and we're going to finish up cold meat.''

"Or hot meat in an iron pot," grinned Lee.

It WASN'T until nearly lunchtime that Dave thought about the rest of the mail.

All the envelopes had been posted within a couple of days of the Big Hit, and each one showed evidence of the attention of the snails. The paper had an unpleasant moist feel, like yesterday's pasta.

There was a reminder from a book club about an unpaid bill from Janine. Pointing out that the charge of twenty-seven dollars and eighty-five cents, including postage, was outstanding for *Thom One* by Mike Howell. Dave vaguely remembered the book arriving, a massive brick of picaresque fiction by "an apocalyptic and star-topping new talent," as the book jacket had advertised.

He threw the bill into the hearth.

There was also a warning that one of their domestic insurance policies was late. Unfortunately the snails had devoured the crucial part of the letter, which would have told Dave what it was for. Since it wasn't likely the company still existed, or would ever pay out another claim, the reminder could safely follow the one from the book club.

Third came a newsletter from Dave's old fraternity at U.C.L.A.—he'd been Phi Beta Kappa—reminding him of a fund-raising exercise for victims of the big floods in Louisiana in the fall of '48.

Last of the four soggy envelopes was a glossy circular that showed a radiant host of men, women and children wandering through a celestial garden in rich robes of gold-threaded silk and with smiles of vacant idiocy on their faces. In the background was a ravaged cinder that Dave assumed was supposed to be Earth.

Dave didn't bother to read which fringe organization of dollar-hunting Christians it had come from. As he crumpled it up, his eyes were caught by the line at the top, in gold mock-Gothic letters. "When the fireball strikes, will you be saved?"

"Yeah," he said. "Yeah, I will."

THE DISCUSSION about *whether* they should go and find Janine, Ellie and Roxanne only took about thirty seconds. Planning the journey and readying the provisions took the better part of two whole days.

Over half of that was spent in the garage, working on their Trackbreaker.

The four-wheel-drive compact truck had stood untouched since the family had left the house. Dave's big worry was that the biting cold had damaged the engine, but it looked in good shape. The dark green paintwork was dusty, with a few old scratches along the flanks. But the powerful overhead-cam V-8 turned smoothly, firing at the second attempt.

One of the biggest problems they faced in using the vehicle was carrying a supply of gas. The chances of finding any on the road were remote, and the journey would be the better part of fifteen hundred miles. The Trackbreaker would do a little over twenty to the gallon on a long highway drive and about three-quarters of that in heavy traffic or cross-country. Since they wouldn't be doing much heavy city driving, it wasn't likely to be a problem.

But that would still leave them needing the full tank of twenty-three gallons plus at least another sixty gallons to reach their destination.

"Can't do it," said Lee, having scavenged all around. "We've got enough cans to hold about twenty-eight spare gallons. And one of the cans hasn't got a proper screw-top. You sure we can drain off the generator fuel, Dad?"

"Sure. Well, we just fill it up to the top and do what we can."

"There's some bottles and stuff."

Dave shook his head. "Not worth it. We're goin' to need them for eating and drinking. She's big inside, but we're going to have her and the trailer full-loaded. Cooking and camping stuff. Ammo and the guns."

"What happens when we run out of gas?" asked the boy.

"We stop," replied the man. "And we'll just have to see what we'll do then."

Before they packed the four-by, they collected everything together into the center of the living room. Each item was checked carefully. Dave had been interested in the survivalist movement for some years, and his knowledge was vital. They had to make sure they had all the essentials.

Compass and maps. Their trusty Aerolyte Wilderness tent. Sleeping bags, now laundered and fresher. Camping stove with every spare cylinder they could find. Water purifying tabs. Spoon and knife, plastic mug and plate each. Couple of pans for cooking.

As many dried-food packets as there were in the house, with every tin off the shelves in the cool larder. Dave was tempted by an unopened bottle of vodka in their liquor cabinet, but reluctantly left it where it was. In the conditions that they were going to face, a depressant that would also multiply the hazards of hypothermia wasn't high on the list of "must-takes."

Clothes were easy. Since the Trackbreaker was fairly spacious, they could pack plenty, including sets of warm clothes for Janine and the girls.

Apart from the truck, they also had the small aluminum trailer that hooked on the back and would hold much of the basic camping gear. One of the tires had a slow leak, and Lee spent an hour with a tub of water trying to find the actual puncture. Eventually he managed to mend it and inflated it with a rusting old foot pump, which was then packed into the trailer in case of emergencies.

It was the emergencies that were difficult to anticipate. Dave went through their comprehensive medicine cupboard, packing what he could into a Nike carryall—various medicines for aches and upsets and coughs. All the plasters and bandages they had, along with a digital thermometer, were also included.

"How about a scalpel and forceps, Dad?" teased Lee, pausing to watch his father.

"If we had them I'd take them," replied Dave. "Long as we keep the wheels moving, we'll be in good shape for supplies. The moment it gives up on us, we're in deep shit."

"Back on the flat of our feet again."

AT LEAST Melmoth was easy to provide for.

In the couple of days since they'd returned home, the pit bull had been visibly uneasy, skulking around in quiet, shadowy corners, as if it knew that all wasn't well. Dave and Lee kept finding the dog lying in one or other of the girls' rooms, looking up expectantly when they entered, then dropping his head again as it realized they weren't either of its young mistresses.

Lee filled a box with the tins of dog food they had and stored it in the trailer.

Apart from the truck, Dave concentrated most of his attention on their weaponry.

Even in the relatively short time since he and Lee had been surviving alone in the bleak and bitter land, it had become obvious that the man who carried the biggest stick was going to have an advantage over his fellows.

Every gun, bow and knife that they possessed was brought into the main living-area and laid out on the carpet. By now the Trackbreaker was more or less packed, ready for an early departure after dawn on the following day. They had each selected their traveling clothes.

One of the great advantages of returning to Cody Heights was that they had been able to draw on their cold-weather supplies. There was no shortage of thermal vests and underwear, warm sweatshirts and waterproof, windproof tops. They'd each packed several pairs of thick socks and gloves, and both were wearing boots with thermal insulation and steel shank, as well as a protective box toe.

Dave found that his wife had left behind her own handgun, a nickel-plated Ruger .32. He'd given her the trim little automatic on their tenth wedding anniversary, after a spate of attacks on women driving alone in the region. Neither of the girls had ever shown any interest in firearms.

"Three hunting bows, Dad? Who's the third one for?"

"Fair chance we might get one damaged in the next few months. Same with the knives."

He had his own much-worn Trail-Master, with the ten-inch blade of finest carbon steel and a nonslip grip of synthetic rubber. Lee had his favorite Blackjack Mamba knife sheathed on his left hip. They also loaded a heavy-duty machete with an eighteen-inch blade and a short-hafted axe.

And the guns.

"Spoiled for choice," said Dave, looking at the array of hardware laid out on the floor in front of them.

Apart from Janine's Ruger, there was a handgun apiece, and likewise a scattergun and rifle. With the Skorpion Mk3 for serious action.

"I'll stick with my good old Beretta Onyx," said Lee. "Never let me down. And the 232 SIG-Sauer pistol."

"How about a rifle?"

Lee looked sideways at his father. "Which rifle are you taking?"

"Why?"

"Well..."

"I don't know. Maybe this bolt-action 941 Sauer. Or the Heckler & Koch G-12 caseless. Difficult to pick up any fresh ammo for that."

"How 'bout the Lux?"

"Ah." He grinned at his son's eagerness. "You always liked that, didn't you?"

"Sure. It's such a real critical-looking piece of action."

Dave lifted the rifle up, weighing it in his hand, feeling the point of balance. The SIG-Sauer 120 Lux had been one of his most expensive buys. He'd picked it up from a used-gun store near San Luis Obispo about eight years before.

It was a classic bolt-action rifle, chambered to take a .458 round in an 8-shot magazine. First on the market in 2025, it was a great hunter's gun, with supreme accuracy and great stopping power. Dave had bought an old Leupold optical sight for it.

He handed it to his son. "You better look after it, Lee."

"Oh, right, Dad. Right."

"I'll stick with the Heckler & Koch with the laser night-scope. That just leaves handguns."

"What about your scattergun?" asked Lee.

"The Browning 12-gauge. And I'll keep my pocket cannon on my hip."

"When can I try firing the Linebaugh, Dad? You said, when I got a bit older."

"Right. When you get a bit older, you can fire the Linebaugh. Don't want you dislocating your wrist or breaking a thumb or anything stupid. Make life hard for both of us, that kind of injury."

"I'll go with that Sauer 9 mm," said the boy. "And that completes what we take. We start tomorrow at dawn."

"Right. We'll put the hardware into the truck just before we go."

THERE WAS another minor quake during the night, rattling the windows. It was clear from the lack of damage around Cody Heights that the region had been spared some of the devastating quakes and eruptions that had destroyed so much of the country.

The shock came around four in the morning, waking both father and son. Since they wanted to make an early start, they got up and enjoyed their last hot baths for a while, then drank coffee together in the warmth of the living room.

"Make the most of this," said Dave. "Guess it'll be quite—"

He was interrupted by the big double window imploding under the impact of a high-velocity bullet.

13

A ten year old girl, Eve Kokack, from Millington, New Jersey, wrote a poem as an entry in a national competition. It was widely republished because of its subject matter. It was also read on the evening news several times in the next few weeks, in early December 2048.

The title of the poem was "My Future."

I love my mom and daddy,
I love my cat called Flix.
I love my own hometown
And me and dad love the Knicks.
I read about a great big star
That's coming here through space.
Though inside I feel frightened
Outside I put on my brave face.
America's faced lots of enemies
In the last three hundred years,
And we've beaten every one of them,
Punched their noses, smacked their ears.
The land of the brave won't run
From a star that's coming near.

We'll all blow a great BIG blow
And send it far from here.
Then Flix and mom and daddy,
The ones I love all three,
Will live on safe for ever,
In our own home of the free.

AROUND FOUR HUNDRED MILES from the epicenter of Adastreia's prime strike, it's unlikely that anyone from Millington, New Jersey, survived for more than a few days.

14

"Hit the lights!" Dave yelled, diving sideways behind a dark green leather armchair, snatching up the Skorpion as he moved.

Lee responded quickly after a moment of frozen shock. He darted toward the door, slapping his hand against the dimmer switch and plunging the room into instant darkness.

"Grab a gun and keep low," ordered Dave, wriggling away from the chair to get next to the window. He squinted into the cold air that came pouring through the shattered glass.

There was a sliver of moon visible through the layers of cloud, giving a poor light across the patio to the frozen pool and the rest of the garden beyond. But there was no sign of movement.

There was an infinite stillness.

Dave was just aware of the lightest of breezes, creeping in from over the Pacific, carrying the hint of salt on its breath. From the room behind him, he heard the panting of Melmoth and knew that the pit bull must have crept in to crouch beside Lee.

"You bastards!" The voice broke the silence, thick with anger.

"You looting bastards in there best come out and face us."

"I know who that is, Dad," whispered Lee. "But I can't just remember."

"We give you a fair trial, you come out and throw out your guns. Come on. We're decent people and we won't have fucking looters."

"It's Mr. Kelly," said Lee.

"The head of your high school! Come on. Mr. Kelly doesn't say 'fucking,' does he?"

"Maybe he does now."

The shouting came again from somewhere among the snow-tipped bushes by the fence. "There's a dozen men here with rifles and shotguns. If you don't come out of Dave Rand's house in one minute from now, then you're all fucking dead meat."

Dave looked at the pale circle of his son's face. "You're right, Lee. He does say 'fucking' now." Raising his voice, he yelled, "That Jeff Kelly out there?"

A long pause followed his words. Then came the demand, "Who's that?"

"Me. David Rand. Lee's here inside with me. And Melmoth."

Outside there was instant confusion. Voices overlapped each other, some claiming to recognize Dave's voice while others suspected a trick. Finally Kelly's commanding tones rose over them all. "Just shut the fuck up, will you?" When it was quiet, he called, "You in there. You reckon to be Dave Rand, do you?"

"Sure. Tell me, what sort of proof you want? We've been out camping. Arizona and New Mexico. Only just got back a couple of days ago. Janine and the girls are up in Montana."

All Dave could hear through the broken window was muttering voices. Then someone else called out. "Dave, if that's you...I'm Paul Crossan and I'm the druggist in Cody Heights. You know me?"

"Yeah. You're *Harry* Crossan, and if you're a druggist, then I'm the worst damned shot in our pistol club."

"It's Dave. By God, it's Dave Rand!"

In a couple of minutes everybody was milling around in the living room, and their departure north was postponed by a few hours while the local vigilante group, all four of them, came in for coffee.

Harry Crossan was a retired shoe salesman who'd settled in Cody Heights ten years before and *was* the worst shot in the local pistol club. Jeff Kelly, the head, came in with his oldest son, Gerry. Both of them held scatterguns. The fourth member of their gang was a tall woman whom Dave didn't know. She was introduced as Melanie Rogers, widow of a state highway patrolman.

Dave was shocked at how the past eighteen months had changed Harry and Jeff. The former had been an independent old codger in his late sixties, always ready to lend a hand in fund-raising, always neat and trim in a subdued three-piece suit, even on the hottest summer afternoons.

Now he was like a raggedy man, his windbreaker torn and patched, the hair dribbling over his shoulders, greasy and matted. A scar across his right cheek looked as if it had been crudely sewed, and Dave noted with a shock that the old man had three fingers missing from his left hand.

Harry saw the shock reflected on the man's face and nodded grimly. "Presume not that I am the thing I was, old friend. Got caught in a bad slide. Jeff here pulled me out, but I lost part of my hand."

Jeff Kelly had once been a stout, amiable man, nudging the scales around two hundred and eighty-five pounds. Dave would have been surprised if the ex-head was anywhere near half of that now. His cheeks had sunken in, and most of his teeth seemed to have gone. And there was a different, wild look in his pale blue eyes.

Their news of what had happened in Cody Heights merely filled in a few details for Dave and Lee, confirming what they'd seen and suspected during the past year and a half.

The first shocks had ravaged the land. Earthquakes that had riven mountains and destroyed whole sections of the township, and eruptions from volcanoes long considered extinct had sent rivers of lava scorching along valleys faster than a man could run.

"Most died, Dave," Jeff said. During the whole of their time together, his son, Gerry, never spoke a word. He never made eye contact but sat silently on the sofa, playing with the cords of his parka.

Harry was more explicit. "There's around twenty still living for thirty miles around," he said grimly. "And most of them are in worse shape than us."

Melanie Rogers nodded wearily. "That's right. There's still places that probably got stuff to live on for a few days. Like your house, Dave. But it's harder and harder to find them, and you have to travel farther and farther. It can't go on for long like this, you know.''

"But there's game here," said Lee. "I've seen tracks everywhere."

Jeff looked at their armory, spread around the room. "Sure, son. If'n you're young and fit and well armed, then you got the patience and the skills to hunt. None of us are much at trailing and hunting. Not anymore."

The house was silent. Melmoth, lying near Dave's feet, growled in his sleep. Through the splinters of the broken window the first light of dawn was already easing across the wooded valley.

"We have to be going," said Dave. "Could you maybe sort of patch up the window so the snow stays outside?"

"Sure. There's been vagrants and looters around in the last month or so." Jeff Kelly scratched the side of his stubbled chin with his finger. "We never knew your place had made it through. Too high and isolated for us. Then we saw the lights and we figured . . ."

Dave nodded. "Yeah. Look, I wouldn't want you all out here trying to protect my property. Lee and I'll get on our way. I'll leave you to lock up and make safe. But help yourself to any food there is. Or anything like that.''

"Thanks, Dave. And if you get back with Jan and the girls, look out for us." The old teacher shook his head, trying unsuccessfully for a smile. "If we're still around, that is.''

Then it was time to go. The Trackbreaker had a powerful and almost silent engine that took them gently away from home. Rolling down the drive, both Dave and Lee waved through the windows at the little group of four standing by their front door.

"Think we'll see 'em again, Dad?"

"I'd like to say we would. But . . .''

The sentence trailed away into the immense whiteness all around them.

ONE OF THE THINGS that Dave had worked on with the truck was trying to make it safer in the event of an attack. There was no way of protecting it from bullets, but he'd found some unused pieces for the chain-link fence in the back of the garage. He had fixed them to the windshield, tailgate and the side windows. It was certainly strong enough to turn a large stone thrown hard—Lee had insisted on giving it a good testing. Dave was a little worried whether the grille over the front might not help snow to build up and obscure vision, but the only way to find out was to use it.

Their plan was to head west, along 178 past Isabella Lake, through Sequoia Forest, through Weldon, then doglegging down onto the old U.S. Highway 395. Proceeding north past Lone Pine, Mammoth Lakes, they'd fork off in the Sweetwaters at Devil's Gate, aiming for Carson City. If they stuck close to 395, it would carry them in more or less the right direction, up through the length of California, through Oregon, into Washington. Then they could find a route to cut back east again, into Montana.

If things went well, Dave had calculated they would run out of gas somewhere around the town of Burns, in central Oregon.

There was a basic conflict that needed to be resolved. If they tried out the main roads, then they were more likely to run into trouble from roving bands. But they might still make better time, with winter already hardening. However, any gas supplies close to the main arteries would have been taken in the first weeks.

The answer was likely to be compromise.

During the first day they made steady progress. After they moved off a highway turned to ribbons of taffy by quakes on a half-dozen separate occasions, their 4x4 picked its cat-footed way over the rough ground. By the time that the light was beginning to fade, hours earlier than it would have done before the Big Hit, they were close to the eastern side of the hills, near to 395. The gray ribbon of the old Los Angeles Aqueduct lay frozen beneath them, sullen and leaden.

They stopped in what had once been a picnic area. The cross-legged benches and tables stood about like a failed exhibition of modern art. The barbecue pits were filled with snow, and the display case showing the local beauty spots and attractions had been smashed.

Forest ranged around for miles. In their day's traveling the only sign they'd seen of any human activity was a thin column of smoke climbing above the pines, far off to their left.

"So far, so good," said Dave, getting out carefully and stretching his legs.

Melmoth leaped to join him, strutting about his new kingdom, anxious for someone or something to challenge him. But the woods were silent, dark and deep.

Lee climbed out, boots crunching in the frozen snow around them. The sky was a familiar dark purple, streaked with pale clouds. The sun had already sunk behind the mountains.

"Think it'll ever get warm again, Dad?" he asked.

"Yeah," replied Dave absently, looking around and trying to take into account the incalculable. Was it safe to light a cooking fire? Somewhere far above them he was conscious of a large bird, swooping beyond the tops of the trees. There was no other sound.

"We going to have a fire?"

"Yes, son, we are."

The other arrangements had been decided upon on the afternoon that they'd begun packing for their odyssey, when Lee had been first to spot the obvious.

"If we can pack the trailer, we can sleep in the truck a lot of times. Keep the tent for when we really need it."

And that was what they'd done, leaving the back seat free for Dave and the front for Lee. Melmoth would have to fit in where he could.

15

"Sunshine Or Shadows?" An edited extract from an NBC special on the approach of the asteroid, transmitted, after government censorship controls, on 30 November 2048.

Rodney Cavendish, New York expert on meteorology: "I think first that we should both say that we are agreed that the risk of any actual contact between this planet and any heavenly body are remote."

Irma Rice, Los Angeles expert on meteorology: "Is."

R.C.: "I'm sorry."

I.R.: " 'Is remote' is correct. You said 'are remote.' I think we should strive for accuracy. And yes, I do agree that the risk is slight. But that doesn't mean it doesn't exist."

R.C.: "My feelings are that any such impact would have very little effect on the environment or the meteo-society, as I like to call it."

I.R.: "I disagree totally. Even a minor impact would trigger a series of effects that would change the weather system of this planet from now until eternity. And beyond."

R.C.: "No. A minor increase in the dust levels of the stratosphere would lower temperatures locally by a couple of degrees for a few months. No worse than an average bad summer or winter."

I.R.: "I had known from reading your published work that you sometimes erred on the side of optimism. I had not realized that you view the future for us all through glasses of absurdly bright rose."

R.C.: "You, I imagine, favor the 'nuclear winter' scenario beloved of the doomsday branch of our science? Well, my dear, it will not happen that way."

I.R.: "Firstly I am emphatically not your dear, Professor Cavendish. Secondly I have little doubt that any impact, however unlikely, could certainly lead to the effective end of life as we know it. There might be a gradual improvement after a year or two, but the damage in human terms will have been done. The deaths will be in billions. Billions!"

R.C.: "Nonsense. There might be some small loss of life in the overcrowded areas of some underdeveloped regions. But that would happen if the crops failed in any year. No. I will not listen to gloom and doom from you. A minor inconvenience for most people. A shade less suntan for the beachies and surfies of your home state, Dr. Rice."

I.R.: "Sadly it is unlikely that we will both survive any potential disaster, so I shall not have the Pyrrhic satisfaction of pointing out the total fallacy of your views. I at least shall die in the certainty of having been proved correct. You will simply go to meet your Maker with the dismal knowledge that you have died a simpleminded old fool!"

16

Dave woke up, stretching the stiffness out of his spine and blinking at the whiteness that surrounded them, blanking out all the windows of the Trackbreaker. He sat up and used the manual override on the window, letting in a gust of clean, cold air, carrying a few flakes of snow with it. Outside there was the evidence of a serious fall during the long hours of darkness. From the height piled up against the legs of one of the picnic tables, Dave Rand guessed it must be over a foot.

"What the dickens...? Oh, didn't know where I was. Hi, Dad. Been snowing?"

"Sure has."

Their voices jerked the pit bull from its canine dreams, and it shook itself awake, sticking its muzzle over the back seat and licking at Dave's hand.

"Wow, close that window, Dad. It's freezing."

"Clearing some of the condensation off of the windows. It's really stuffy in here. How d'you sleep, Lee?"

"Yeah," came the hesitant answer. "Still have some critical bad dreams."

"Me, too."

"Really?"

"Course."

"What about? Mom and the girls? Kind of bad dreams about them. I had this one where we were all on holiday and they were on a cliff, way above us. The rock had a big split, clean down it, and it was ready to fall. You and me were trying to warn them, but they couldn't hear us. Just kept on waving and smiling. Smiling a lot."

Dave patted the boy on the shoulder. "I know son, I know. Kind of dreams I get, too."

"Come on, Dad. Close that window. It'll freeze my balls off."

"Lee," he said warningly. "You wouldn't talk like that in front of your mother. So don't talk like it now."

But he wound the window shut, and in a short while they were already on the roll.

The highway toward Lone Pine was in good shape—better than anything that they'd seen. The sun came crawling up, and the temperature rose to just a little below freezing. The pavement was mainly swept clear by the biting winds, leaving it coated with a dusting of snow over a layer of sheet ice. Driving was infinitely treacherous and required enormous concentration.

Lee hadn't got a license when they left California on their camping trip, but Dave had already begun giving him some lessons. It became obvious by midmorning that their progress would be much better if they both drove.

The truck had an automatic box with a manual override facility providing the driver with extra-low-gears and a special low reverse for really hard terrain. For the time being, Dave ignored them and concentrated simply on teaching Lee how to use the straight automatic gearing. With no other traffic anywhere on the road and decent visibility, it made the lesson relatively easy.

"Just go easy on the pedals, Lee. Slow and easy. Press too hard, and you'll start to lose the rear end. And if you begin to slide, then steer into it. Keep the speed around twenty."

"It'll take us years to reach Montana at that speed!" protested the boy.

"We come off the highway into a culvert, and there's no tow truck rushing to help us out. That way we'd probably never reach Montana," Dave reminded him, and Lee's protest stopped.

The mountains stretched out on their left as they moved steadily northward. Once they saw a ragged child, shrouded in a patchwork of furs, standing watching them from the porch of an abandoned gas station. Dave was at the wheel of the Trackbreaker, and he slowed right down. The little girl stopped sucking her thumb and vanished into the whitewashed building. Almost immediately a scrawny woman came out, oddly wearing only a sleeveless shirt and cut-off jeans. She held what looked like an M-16 carbine.

Dave pressed down on the accelerator and eased them away from any threat. He watched the woman in the rearview mirror, standing quite still. When the truck rounded a curve, a mile farther on, she hadn't moved.

Melmoth stood on the rear seat, bracing himself against the movement of the vehicle, looking eagerly out. Once they passed a small herd of deer, and he started to bark. Lee glanced across at his father, who shook his head.

"Not here. Should be plenty of game as we get further north."

In the next hour they glimpsed a middle-sized grizzly, with a great hump of silver-tipped fur, standing over the bloodied corpse of a deer. It looked up suspiciously at the noise of the engine, but showed no sign of retreating.

"I reckon we could make it by hunting, you know, Dad," Lee said.

"As long as we didn't finish up being the ones hunted," Dave replied.

Early afternoon found them with a major rockslide blocking the road. The actual surface of the highway had been torn apart by a quake, leaving a crevasse that seemed bottomless. Lee had been driving, but his father took the wheel from him. Engaging the lowest gear he picked his way cautiously around the shoulder and over the rocky land to the right.

It took them an hour to cover less than three miles, but finally they were able to get back on the road again.

"That a store over there?" Dave asked, pointing to the east side of 395. A rectangular building was visible, its roof covered in snow. At a distance it looked surprisingly as though it was untouched by either nature or man.

Dave spun the wheel, and they pulled into a massive parking lot filled with the ghostly shapes of abandoned shopping carts scattered everywhere, rusting and silent.

"Glass looks broke," Lee observed, lowering his window and peering out.

"Might as well stretch our legs awhile. Give Melmoth a chance to do whatever it is a dog has to do."

The pit bull didn't need any encouragement, diving down, his stumpy legs skidding on the gray ice. He looked around him, then cocked a contemptuous leg against a light pole.

"You've got the SIG-Sauer pistol, Lee? Keep it ready."

"No sign of life here. No tracks. Nothing."

The impression they'd had of the store from a distance was clearly false. Now that they stood close up to it, they could see the long front window had been smashed, probably by one of the countless quakes.

"Have a look inside?" suggested the boy. "Might be something left in there."

Inside was nothing but bleak desolation.

Father and son walked together along the endless silent aisles, rubbish crunching under their boots. The light filtered in from outside, making the store seem like a vast undersea grotto.

Dave stopped at the end of the rows marked by signs advertising Canned Goods and Pet Products. "God, Lee, this all makes me feel kind of like a traveler just stepped out of his time machine."

"Looks like everything's been taken that might be any use."

"Yeah. It figures. No point in wasting time in here."

One of the odd things was that there were a few sections that had hardly been disturbed, while others were totally empty.

The shelves of household goods were largely untouched. Dusty bottles of bleach and drain cleaners. Armies of tins of polish and preservatives. Piles of dusters and cloths. The aisle of summer clothes were still as they'd been, though the parts of the store that had sold food and drink were stripped bare.

"If we'd been characters in a book," said Lee, "there'd have been a stockpile of food that everybody had somehow missed and we'd find it. Like a secret attic in a rambling old house."

"Yeah. But we're not, and there isn't."

Dave found an audio tape of Dvořák's *New World* Symphony and picked it up out of the rubbish. But when he came to try it in the truck's sound system, the thin tape spooled out noiselessly. So much for the new world, he thought wryly.

So they pressed on. A little farther north, and they reached the fringe of the most devastated area

THE AMERICAN EAGLE—A symbol of freedom, courage and justice for all.

THE GOLD EAGLE—A symbol of gripping adventure reading that just doesn't quit.

And in 1991, Gold Eagle brings you more of the raw action and electrifying adventure you've come to expect. Introducing four brand-new series . . .

they'd ever encountered. Fallen trees lay on the flanks of the mountains to their left, stripped of branches and bark, like the tumbled columns of a vast Greek temple. And there were lakes of leprous-looking gray mud everywhere, frozen solid, with seams and cracks breaking up the smooth surface.

"Must have been an eruption off west," said Dave, slowing the vehicle to a gentle pace. "Steam and pumice and all that shit."

"Like a forest fire. We saw that up in Glacier once."

"Yeah. But worse. I read someplace about what it's like. The side bursts open of a mountain and all this stuff comes gushing out. Superheated steam and fragments of rock going around seven hundred miles an hour. Like a boiler exploding."

Lee gasped. "Seven hundred miles an hour! That's double critical, Dad. It'd kill everything in its path, wouldn't it?"

Dave stared out of the driver's window. "Looks like it did."

By late afternoon they were close to Lone Pine. It was a small town, built around the main street, with a gas station, several stores and a few eateries. A gaggle of motels stood together at its southern end, totally silent and abandoned. Large trees lined the highway, most of them already dead or dying.

Lee was driving, gradually becoming more relaxed at the wheel.

"Dad!"

Dave had dozed off in the passenger seat, his head resting on his hand. At Lee's call, he started awake, yawning, turning it into a muffled cough. "What is it?" he asked, rubbing his eyes.

The boy eased off the accelerator, slowing again to less than ten miles per hour. "Someone up ahead, Dad."

There were two... no, three figures, standing together on the side of the road, about two hundred yards in front of them. They weren't moving at all, the white splashes of their faces turned toward the oncoming vehicle. For a moment Dave remembered how clusters of students would take to the highways at the beginnings of summer vacations. He'd generally stop for the hitchhikers.

"They look like they want a lift."

"No," Dave snapped.

"Dad, they..." The Trackbreaker eased down below five miles an hour as Lee searched for an argument.

The figures had moved slightly, as if they anticipated being given a lift. Dave leaned across and stamped his boot down on top of his son's foot, making the truck jerk forward. Simultaneously locks slammed home on the doors.

"Hey!" exclaimed Lee, snatching at the wheel, making the four-by veer right across the far side of the highway.

Dave caught a glimpse of three faces that looked painfully young. Thin and drawn, eyes sunken, mouths open in expressions of disappointment as they saw their hopes dashed by the truck's acceleration.

Lee turned to face him. "Get your fucking boot off mine, will you?"

"Lee, we don't know..."

He took his foot off, allowing Lee to bring the vehicle back to a more gentle, controlled speed. Dave had never seen such flaring anger in his son's face, and it shocked him.

"We don't know what, Dad? They were three kids, that's all. They looked stranded and hungry and cold, and we just drive on by."

"There's three of them, and they could maybe try and take us over. Kill us."

He looked back, where Melmoth was standing on the rear seat, eagerly watching the shrinking figures behind them.

Lee was calmer, but still angered. "Dad. One of them could have been me. Or Ellie or Roxie. Couldn't they?"

Dave took a long slow breath. "Yeah, okay, son. Turn around. Let's go back."

17

From the 3 December edition of the Washington Post*, headlined by 'Thousands Of Chinese Die In Asteroid Riots.'*

Reports reaching the west through the New China News Agency, based in the former British colony of Hong Kong, are beginning to reveal the story of a huge death toll. Riots among frightened peasants in the Hainan Tibetan Autonomous Prefecture, centered on Tanyemu Province, are reported to have been sparked by an official government statement, emanating from Beijing, suggesting that rogue asteroid, Adastreia, could possibly strike mainland China.

The initial warning attempted to play down any implications of serious threat, but still succeeded in causing panic on a large scale. Provincial police forces, supported by a battalion of the regular army who were engaged in exercises nearby, tried to disperse the rioters.

Some onlookers put the numbers in the demonstrations as high as half a million, though government sources deny this figure. Reports also state that the gathering was mainly peaceful, relying only on banners and the chanting of slogans calling upon the central government to take action to remove the fearsome "circle of burning sky" from them. It was only when the military, without apparent warning, began to open fire that the demonstration turned into a riot.

Official sources claim that "a few troublemakers and revisionist running curs" have been injured and taken prisoner. Western spectators suggest figures for the dead could be as high as fifty thousand—mostly in and around the main cities.

Martial law has been declared, and tanks patrol the deserted, curfew-controlled streets.

A spokesman for the United States Department of Defense-Astronomy in Washington refused to make any comment on increasing domestic fears fueled by the approaching asteroid. He simply said that a statement would be issued when considered appropriate.

18

The Inyo Lawns Resting Place was situated in a quiet meadow, four miles to the west of the main highway. It nestled among the foothills of the Sierra Nevada, alongside what once had probably been a skillfully sculptured river that tinkled over white pebbles between grassy banks.

Now it was mainly iced-up, with just a fast-flowing stream keeping a narrow passage open at its center. The bushes on both sides had become encrusted with clear ice, making them look like fragile capillaries of spun crystal.

The gnawed carcass of a large elk was frozen near the far bank with a nest of animal tracks trampled into the snow around it. There were also innumerable fallen trees trapped and tangled in the ice piles. From a rift somewhere higher up, a hot spring had been released, and it had flowed down to join the river, leaving a trail of delicate sulphur flowers like a golden gash across the bare rock.

The massive stone arch over the entrance had its deeply incised letters picked out with a dusting of powdery snow. The iron gates stood wide apart, revealing the long curved driveway leading up to the main concentration of buildings. Here and there a few memorials stood out among the expanse of white, reminding Dave of a visit he'd once paid as a teenager to the Custer Battlefield on the Little Bighorn. A Soldier Of The 7th Cavalry. June 25, 1876. That was his memory of the simple granite tablets.

The covering of ice and snow on the driveway was utterly virginal, looking like nothing had traveled along it in the past eighteen months.

Melmoth wasn't taking too kindly to being relegated to the tailgate section of the truck and had begun a steady, low snarling.

"Your pit bull won't attack us, will he, Mr. Rand?"

"Not unless you give him good cause, Phil."

Lee was in the passenger seat, and he turned around and told the dog to keep quiet. "He's fine. Just that he hasn't seen any strangers in the last year and a half, so he's kind of edgy."

The boy grinned a gap-toothed smile. "Guess we're all a touch edgy, good buddy."

"We stopping here for the night, Mr. Rand?" asked the younger girl.

"Looks solid enough and safe enough. Unless it's been damaged, we should find somewhere out of the wind. You aren't bothered about sleeping in a graveyard, are you, Carrie?''

She shrugged her shoulders. "Guess not. No, I'm not."

The older girl, Zera, who said she was nearly eighteen, brushed her tousled blond hair away from her face and leaned forward, tapping Lee on the shoulder. "You like splatter-vids? Well-major, aren't they?"

The light was fading fast, but Dave could have sworn that his son was blushing.

None of the three had a second name. Phil, Carrie and Zera. They said they came from Los Angeles, but they became vague when Dave asked them what part of the city. They were also vague about quite what they were doing trying to hitch a lift out on Highway 395 when the world was almost totally lacking cars.

"Been shooting the hog around here for a few months," said Phil. He was around twenty years old, with a scrubby beard and long hair tied back in a yellow bandanna. He wore jeans and a thermal vest and was packing minimal food supplies along with a sleeping bag.

He and Carrie had been together for a year or so, but Zera had only joined them a few days ago. All three of them had been devotees of hi-board riding, like Lee, and much of their talk contained elements of the sport's esoteric slang.

Carrie was seventeen with spiky red hair. Her clothes were identical to Phil's. Dave guessed they'd probably looted the same clothes store. Unlike Phil, she rarely let a word go past her lips.

Zera was a little more forthcoming about herself. She'd been at college, majoring in sports meditation, and had dropped out the Christmas before the Big Hit. She was around five-ten, with a fresh complexion and rough-cropped blond hair. Her eyes, Dave noticed, were a startling blue.

They claimed to be weaponless, apart from a hunting knife, snapped halfway along the blade, that Phil produced.

After the short break at home in Cody Heights, Dave Rand had become much more sensitive about personal freshness. All three of the hikers stank, but he realized that within a few days, he and Lee would once again smell very much the same.

THE INYO LAWNS RESTING PLACE was a perfect spot to pass a night in relative comfort and security. After Phil and Carrie offered to take charge of the cooking, they scavenged around in the dusk and came back with armfuls of dried branches for a fire. In a small, sheltered courtyard with the dried-up remnants of a carp pond in one corner, they made their fire. The high walls kept off the wind and also hid the light of the blaze from any curious eyes in the country beyond.

Melmoth stayed close to Lee's heels as he walked with Dave and Zera through the echoing, vaulted corridors of the complex of ceremonial death.

"What's an ossuary, Dad?" Lee asked, pointing to a skewed notice in black Gothic lettering on a wall.

"Something to do with bones, I think. Maybe where they kept the bones before they crushed them up and put them into the urns."

"How much is a North Dakota urn?" queried Zera.

"I don't know," replied Dave, then came back gamely with "How much *is* a North Dakota urn?"

"Fifty dollars a week less than you earn in South Dakota."

"Oh, I get it," Lee grinned. "It's a sort of a joke."

The girl smiled. "Yeah. Sort of."

They wandered on, continuing their unconducted tour, past the Golgotha Memorial Chapel and the Annunciation Sculpture Grotto. Then they went through the Caskets of Many Ages Display, taking a detour to check out the Last Supper Snack and Fillers. But others had been there before them, and the place was stripped bare as a pauper's larder.

"Think Melmoth would like to pay a visit to Fur and Feather Valley?" asked Zera, stooping to pat the pit bull on the back. He responded with a rumbling snarl.

"Looks like he's not keen. Boy, this is one of the damnedest places I ever did come across." Dave shook his head. "Maybe the asteroid did a little good if it put this out of business."

"Trade must have been great in the first days after the Hit," suggested Lee.

"No. I reckon that those who survived the first impact would have been too busy scratching for food to worry about placing their dear departed in a Disneyland for the Sleeping Americans. Don't you think?"

By the time they got back, the cans of stew and mixed vegetables were simmering nicely on the porta-stove. They ate greedily, then lolled around the cheery fire.

Phil looked over at Dave. "You got a shit-lot of blasters," he said, leaning back on his stained sleeping bag alongside the embers.

"We got enough."

"What's that rocket launcher on your hip, there? Biggest keying pistol I ever saw. What is it? Super-Magnum?"

"Linebaugh .475. Yeah, it's sort of big."

"Wish we had guns, Phil baby," said Carrie, who was lying alongside him, her head resting in his lap. "We should've taken that old scattergun from the woman up in—"

"Shut your fat lips, will you? Told you. Don't want to bore Dave and Lee here with the dumb things we've done the last few months."

She pulled a face at him, then tugged his hand down and pressed it noisily to her lips.

"Think we should have someone to watch, Dave?" asked Zera.

He shook his head, suddenly aware of how tired he felt after two days of driving. "There weren't any signs in the snow. You see anything when you got the wood, Phil?"

"No. Few dog tracks was all. What's the sleeping arrangements?"

"Me and Lee in the van. You three here, around the fire. Might be a good idea to get some more kindling for it. Last the night. It's getting way under freezing already."

"We got the last lot. How 'bout you and Lee getting some this time?"

"Our food. Our truck. You want wood, son, then you get it."

Dave saw the flash of anger, sparking deep in Phil's eyes, but it was quickly hidden, locked away behind a broad smile. "Sure, boss. Forgot that for a moment. C'mon, Zera. Give a hand."

The girl stood up. "Sure."

When Dave and Lee were snugly in the Trackbreaker, the fire was blazing brightly once more.

"Lee," said Dave quietly.

"What is it, Dad?"

"Check all the doors are locked."

"Hey, you don't think that—"

"Just do like I say, Lee. Do it."

THE NIGHT PASSED without any sort of disturbance. When Dave woke up, it was to find Zera stooped over the cooking pot, brewing up some coffee. Phil was nowhere in sight, but Carrie was hunched in her sleeping bag, playing with what looked like a pile of shards of colored glass.

Dave unwound himself, rubbing the sleep from the corners of his eyes. The trouble with having had sudden access to hot water and soap meant that now he realized how dirty he was becoming. The inside of the Nissan smelled like a bear's armpit.

"What you got there?" he asked the girl as he crouched by the fire and helped himself to the fresh brew.

"Glass. Pretty, isn't it? Phil went early and got it for me. He knows that I like real pretty things like this."

Dave reached out and picked up a loose handful, careful not to cut himself on the splintered edges. Behind him he heard Lee clamber out of the truck and go out around the corner to relieve himself.

The glass was unusually thick, with rich, deep colors. Azure and cobalt. Crimson and emerald green. Turquoise and aquamarine. Some of the pieces seemed to have paint on them.

"These are from a window, aren't they?" Dave asked, holding one piece to the light of the fire, admiring the warmth of the tint.

"Sure. I said I liked it, so Phil went and broke it all up. A picture of Jesus beating the shit out of some guys with long beards in a kind of a temple or something."

"That was a real nice stained window," said Dave, unable to hide his shock. "You mean he smashed that in, just so's you could have some pretty glass to play with?"

"Sure. Why not? Phil breaks anything he don't like," she said, smiling up at him, the light from the fire showing the nest of sores around the corners of her mouth.

Zera came to offer him a mug of coffee, keeping one eye on Carrie while she spoke to him. "I'd be kind of careful about criticizing Phil, if I were you, Dave. He doesn't—"

"You aren't me, Zera! I hate wanton, aimless vandalism. I always did in the old days, and I still do now. It's not like breaking up things to burn because you need a fire. It's just..."

Lee appeared, finishing zipping up his jeans, pausing as he saw and heard his father's anger. "What's wrong, Dad?"

"You know that beautiful window we saw yesterday when we were walking around?"

"Which one?"

"Christ driving the moneylenders out of the temple. Well, our hitcher friend has gone and knocked the fuck out of it just for a laugh!"

Zera laid a hand on the arm of the furious man. "I've only been with them a little, but you have to be careful."

Dave looked into the young woman's eyes, shaking his head and sighing, trying to control his temper. Suddenly, shockingly, he saw her eyes change, widen with surprise at something she'd seen behind him. Even before her mouth opened to call a warning, he was already starting to turn, filled with the sickening realization that, whatever it was, he was going to be way too late for it.

He caught the beginnings of a yell from Lee, then his whole head was filled with an overwhelming crack. Even as he went down, Dave was managing to work out that the noise must have been a length of two-by-four that Phil had broken off somewhere. It had hit him part on the shoulder and part on the side of the skull. If he hadn't spotted that warning in Zera's eyes, the full force of the blow would have come across the back of his head.

Someone was rolling him over and fumbling at his belt. Dave knew that he should be trying to struggle, but all he wanted to do was lie on his back and admire the light-pink-and-white clouds that streaked the dawn sky.

Lee was shouting something, and he could hear the two young women screaming. Dimly there was the noise of a dog barking.

"Melmoth," he muttered, wondering why the pit bull hadn't come to his rescue. Part of his scrambled brain decided that the animal must still be locked in the vehicle.

"Dad!"

"Get back, you little jerk-off! And you, Zera! Keep the fuck out my fucking way."

Dave managed his attention on what was happening, half sitting up. The kid with the yellow bandanna around his greasy hair had successfully coldcocked him. He was standing with his back to the fire, with the girl—what was her name? Carrie—at his side. Lee was facing him, ten paces away, fists clenched. The other young woman was just watching. And Phil had a gun in his hand.

"I thought you didn't..." Dave began, then he realized what the gun was. His own Linebaugh, ripped away from his holster while he was on the ground.

"Phil..." Zera began, but the skinny youth waved the massive pistol at her, holding it negligently in his right hand.

"Shut it. You've been a double-crit pain since we ran together. Looks like we part here. Me an' Carrie'll go alone."

The light of the fire reflected off an open razor that had magically appeared in the hand of the redhead. She was grinning happily at what was going down, and Dave Rand realized, to his surprise, that he was going to get killed. So was the woman Zera, and his only son, Lee. And there wasn't too much he could do about it.

"Throw your truck keys over here, Dave, good buddy." The gaping muzzle of the Linebaugh drifted in his direction.

"Fuck you, you dead-eyed little heap of cold shit."

"You what—?"

Dave could see the finger already whitening on the trigger. "You deaf-as-well, you cockless—"

The boom of the .475 was deafening in the enclosed courtyard.

Dave Rand closed his eyes.

19

TOP SECRET. Totality Security Memo, Clearance Levels 19 and above ONLY. From Def-Ast to Chiefs Allsec. 10 December 2048.

Most recent comp-preds now show a prob-factor of more than 38% of severe impact of the rogue asteroid Adastreia with Earth. The megacull potential has likewise increased from the reported figure of 6.85% on 15/11/48. It is now calculated as being in excess of 22%.

This increase, in less than four weeks, gives some cause for concern. These figures have a stat-fail parameter of plus or minus 10%, depending on the improving accuracy of the astronomical observations. Put at its simplest, the closer that Adastreia comes to our planet, the easier it will become to predict if or when and where it will impact.

The very best comp-preds indicate that the likely date for near-prox of the asteroid is around 12 January. Location predictions are impossible due to the probability that there will be some degree of fragmentation as it explodes through our atmosphere.

Level 6 contact with all others, friendly or not, is now being maintained. Stellar missile experts from many others and from our people are working together to look at the optimum scenario effect needed to break up and destroy Adastreia if it should be deemed necessary to do so.

There is a strong majority view that the public, here and elsewhere, should be kept from concern on this matter. To this end it has been agreed that steps will be taken to embargo relevant news items and, in extreme circumstances, arrange for hostile personalities to be silenced.

P.S. Further on this for 22 and Above ONLY from Cent Int Ex Proj.

ENDS.

20

The bullet from the Linebaugh took a little over one-hundredth of a second to travel from Phil to Dave.

Not even a moment to blink. By the time Dave Rand opened his eyes again, the bullet had already smashed into the stone wall four feet above his head and a yard to the left.

He saw a strangely frozen tableau, similar to a second or so earlier yet bizarrely different.

Lee was where he'd been, but his reflexes were fast enough that he'd already started moving toward the parked truck, after his own gun. And Melmoth.

Zera hadn't moved, but stood gaping at Phil. Carrie was doing the same, her jaw dropped as if she'd just been kicked in the stomach.

And Phil? The very Phil, who'd just pulled the trigger of the big handgun, certain as he did so that he was executing the lean, middle-aged man who sat on the ground five paces away from him.

Things had changed for Phil.

Totally unprepared for the kick of the immensely powerful gun, Phil had failed to brace his right wrist with his left hand. As a result the recoil had broken his right wrist, dislocated his thumb and jerked back so hard that the foresight had opened his forehead to the bone. Blood streamed down his face over his eyes, while the Linebaugh fell from his limp fingers to land, ringing on the stone-flagged floor.

He didn't yell, or scream or curse, but just stood there gagging on the pain. As Dave got to his feet, the young man doubled over, puking as a thin string of yellow bile splattered his jeans. He made a feeble effort to mop the blood from the deep gash in his temple, while also holding his broken wrist with his left hand.

"What'd you do, you prick?" screeched Carrie, taking a hesitant half step toward Dave, the razor weaving an uncertain circle in the air in front of her.

"Nothing. Did it himself," he replied.

Zera was close to the redheaded girl, and simply half turned to chop at her arm with the flattened edge of her palm. Carrie cried out, and the razor tinkled on the stones.

"Thanks," Dave said, stooping and picking up the fallen Linebaugh, avoiding the spreading pool of Phil's blood and vomit.

Preceded by a snarling Melmoth, Lee reappeared, holding the scattergun. Even at that moment of extreme tension, Dave was pleased to see that his son had picked the sensible weapon option.

"Dad! You okay? Heel, Melmoth, heel!" The psyched-up pit bull was anxious to launch itself at the stopped, bleeding figure.

"Yeah, fine. Keep the girl covered."

"Both the bitches?"

"No!" Dave exclaimed, louder than he'd intended, shock riding his voice. "No. Zera knocked away the razor." Then came the second thought. "Well, just take care, Lee."

"What happens now?" asked Zera, licking her lips nervously.

"Let us go, Mr. Rand," Carrie said, still rubbing her bruised arm.

Phil had straightened, finally letting the blood have its way. It poured over his eyes, trickled over the narrow nose and in and out of the mouth. Finally it dribbled off the end of his chin.

Coughing, he shook his head. "Just let us go, Dave. I'm fucked."

Dave was suddenly aware of the great abyss that split his character. Eighteen months ago a scene like this would have been a melodramatic nightmare. If it had happened then, he'd have behaved in a civilized way and turned the couple over to the sheriff's department.

Eighteen months was a lifetime.

"You're going to let them go, aren't you, Dave?" asked Zera. "Come on, there's a moral imperative here and sanctity of life. I know they might have been trying to—"

"Might! Don't talk to me about moral imperatives. I want none of that shit. We aren't in that world anymore. Now we're in a world where people try to kill others. And if they fail, then…" He allowed the words to slide away.

"Dad, can we talk, please?"

"Lee, remember our family saying? That talk is cheap but—"

"The price of action is colossal. Yeah, I know that."

"Pack the four-by. Load everything in and then get her started. Put Melmoth in. Zera, you help him."

For a long moment the only sound was the crackling of the breakfast fire and Phil's heavy, choked breathing. Lee looked at his father uncertainly.

At last he nodded. "And you'll be along?"

"Right. And leave me the Onyx."

Lee handed him the over-and-under shotgun and began to tidy up the campsite. After a brief hesitation, Zera began to help him. Carrie moved to put her arm around Phil, who'd just begun to cry.

It took only five minutes to clean up and load everything. When it was finished, Lee grabbed Melmoth by the collar and took him to the truck. Zera stood for a moment, looking at Phil and Carrie, then at Dave, standing with the shotgun cradled in his arms.

"No point in my saying anything to you, is there?" she asked him. Taking the shake of the head for her answer, she said, "Thought not."

She vanished, heels clicking on the flags, and a few moments later Dave heard the engine cough to life.

Still bleeding heavily and obviously concussed, the young man had slipped to his knees, clutching his broken wrist. Carrie stood at his side, one hand on his shoulder, her face turned defiantly to Dave.

"You just going to drive off and leave us to starve, you bastard?"

"No."

The flat syllable penetrated, and she shook Phil. "Listen, baby. Hear him!"

Dave brought the Beretta up to his shoulder, sighting along the steel barrel. His finger edged down onto the single selective trigger, taking up the first pressure.

"No, mister, no," gabbled the girl. "You gotta listen to me and . . ."

"No," he said very gently. "There's no more time."

At close range the steel shot hardly starred out at all. The first round struck Carrie in the side of the head as she started to turn away, and the second drove into the top of the skull of the kneeling boy.

Dave stared, unseeing, at the two twitching, kicking bodies flailing in a lake of bright blood. Then he turned and rejoined the others.

THEY MOVED ON NORTH, Lee at the wheel, in absolute silence for nearly an hour. The only sound was the humming of the heavy-duty tires on the rutted ice and packed snow of the highway. It was a beautiful morning with a hazy sun appearing through banks of low cloud that clung to the tops of the Sierras, over to their left.

Finally it was the young woman who broke the long silence between them. "I'm sorry I was traveling with them," she said. "Real sorry."

Dave was in the passenger seat, and he turned around to face her, seeing that Melmoth had crept forward from the tailgate and was half lying on her lap.

"You can pick a lot of things in life, and a lot you can't. Family you can't pick. But you can be careful how you choose friends. And the way civilization—if you can still call it that—the way it is now, I think you've got to be even more careful. Don't you, Zera?"

"I know that. There was something spooky and... I was truly total. Out there it's sometimes better to go around with a homicidal maniac than on your own. Know what I mean?"

Lee spoke for the first time in more than twenty miles of driving. "You did kill them both, didn't you, Dad?"

"I did. You know...Christ I *hope* you know...I didn't *want* to execute them. But if I'd have left them alive, then they could've preyed on someone else. That was why."

"If this big softy got bitten by a bat with rabies...you'd put him down?" Zera ruffled the short hairs at the nape of the pit bull's muscular neck. "Would you, Dave?"

"Sure."

ZERA HAD BEEN in San Bernardino during the days immediately after the Hit. She had barely managed to get away from the cluster of communities before society completely collapsed.

She told them what it had been like as they sat around a blazing fire a couple of nights later. Dave had taken a narrow side road, picking his way through banks of high snow, eventually finding a secure camping site for them in the grounds of an ecumenical college.

"There were some real bad times. I know you got this plan to get north and then cut east. And I kind of understand about needing speed to reach your family quick."

Dave read the unspoken "but" in what she was saying. "You got a better plan?" he asked.

She shook her head. "Not for me to say, Dave. I ride with you and eat your food. Not for me to shove in my five cents' worth."

"That's a pile of shit, Zera! One thing I've learned about life now is that none of the old rules apply anymore. You're with us, and you're with us all the way. In trouble you fight with us. Maybe you'll end up having to die with us. You have the right to say just what you want.''

"Your route takes us through Reno and—'' she paused to check the Rand McNally on her lap "—Carson City. There's a road off to the east. Well, it's lots of little roads. Takes us up to Yellowstone Park in the end. But that's not far from Montana, is it?''

"Show me,'' said Dave, and Lee moved to peer over his shoulder.

"Here, Toiyabe National Forest. Up to Alternate 95. Four four seven up to Black Rock Desert. See?''

"Yeah. Worth a try. What do you think, Lee? Better route?''

The boy nodded. "Tell us a bit more about the city.''

"It was madness, Lee. I mean *real* madness. Hundreds dying of thirst in their homes and in the streets. Pet animals eating the bodies. Rats out of the sewers. Fires burning all over the city. Lots of folks chilled themselves out.''

"I heard about that,'' Dave said with a nod. "Guns, sleepers, razors.''

"Ropes, bridges, plain old plastic bags. All they were doing was getting some sort of control over their way of going.''

Lee looked at the map, angling it to try and read the fine print by the firelight. "Sounds like cities are real key places to shoot the duck around. Must have been a high-funk smell with all those bodies around."

Zera smiled at him. "Don't sked off on that hi-line, Lee. Don't forget that in January the sun shines a whole lot in California. Out near the Mojave. On the day of the Smash, it was in the seventies. Temperatures didn't fall like a stone. Took days to slither down into the winter we got now."

Dave took the map off his son and stared at it. Shaking his head doubtfully, he remarked, "Could be hard to find gas off the main highways." He sucked at the small hole in a back tooth where a tough piece of deer meat had popped out a filling. "Then again, I suppose that the side trails could be the ones that nobody's bothered to look at."

"Truck'll use more gas off the highway," Lee offered.

"How long will it take us to reach Montana?" asked Zera, reaching to help herself to another bowl of the canned soup.

"How long's a length of rope? It might be we'll find a whole mountain's shifted and blocked off any hope of driving another mile. Might be we can just roll along the blue highways, finding gas when and where we want it. No marauding bands of crazies trying to kill us. Who knows? Melmoth here knows just about as much as we do.''

The dog's stumpy little tail wagged as it recognized its name.

The young woman began to laugh at the eager response. Lee also started laughing, followed some seconds later by Dave.

It was a rare good moment.

21

The Church of Tomorrow's Golden Tabernacle. From the Christmas Appeal, 2048.

Brothers and sisters, old and young, healthy or afflicted, rich or poor! Friends!

This is your counselor, the Very Reverend Gordy Newman, from Tulsa, Oklahoma, coming calling on you... and you and you. Coming with my begging bowl outstretched once more, for you to fill it brimfully overflowing in your generosity as you have always done in our special appeal to coincide with the Nativity of our Saviour, Himself.

In the last few weeks many of you out there have been asking me after our television and radio appearances the answer to the Big question in everyone's mind right now.

"Rev Gordy," you say. "What about this big old asteroid that's supposed to be coming our way?" You want to know two things. Will it hit us, and is it the manifestation of God's wrath against us earthly sinners?

Good questions, friends.

They call this Adastreia "The Inescapable." Well, I say "Hogwash!" There's nothing in this world or in the blessed afterlife in Paradise the golden and eternal that's inescapable. I've pored through the Good Book night after night on your parts, searching for a clue from the Almighty about His intentions. And I can't find a single word about any collision between us and an old bit of a planet.

So, here's Gordy's answers to those two questions. No, it won't hit us. Anyone says otherwise, then you refer them to Gordy.

But the other question's a tad more difficult. It may well be that this inescapable asteroid is a *warning*. It's like a note to your local store that he's been hiking prices up on cornbread too high. Maybe we ought to all think about dropping our prices to the land of darkness. Look for the light and live in the way of the Golden Tabernacle of Tomorrow. All call out, together, "Hallelujah!"

Bless you.

Now, those of you on the standard monthly tithing, paid by standing orders, have to do nothing extra. Less'n you want to, says Gordy. The Christmas surcharge will slip in on your account, and you won't hardly feel the pain!

The rest of you good folks out there can dip into your conscience first and your wallets second. Remember that you'll never get the best of a better man. And a better man needs the best.

The address for the mailings is at the head of this appeal.

And don't worry about Adastreia. Let Rev. Gordy, and God, do all that worrying for you.

Bless you all, and let your dollars keep the prayer wheels spinning.

Merry Christmas!

22

It was a help having Zera take her share of the driving chores.

Since the daylight period was sometimes shortened by bitter storms, it meant pressing on as long and hard as they could on the better days.

Dave Rand had lost track of the precise date, but he guessed that it must be early September. His problem had been compounded by a whiteout that had stopped them, tucked into the lee of an abandoned warehouse. They were trapped there for three or four days, unable to drive and unable to get out for more than a few minutes at a time. Cooking was impossible, and the constant screaming of a hundred-mile-per-hour wind tugged at their nerves.

But when the storm had petered out, they stretched their limbs and continued on.

Gas had begun to run low as they neared the Idaho state line.

One of the tires had given out as they'd battled over a rutted, high ridge, and the front left tire was thin where the tracking had been knocked irreparably out of alignment while avoiding some fallen trees in a forest valley in the Oregon wilderness.

But despite the hard knocks, the four-by still started up every morning and carried them on through the day.

One thing that surprised Dave was how few people there seemed to be left in the country. Allowing for the fact that they had chosen to travel the back roads and narrow trails, they rarely saw another human being from one dawn to the next.

During the long drive since they'd left Cody Heights, they'd only encountered about a dozen other gas-powered vehicles. Most had been at a distance, but there had been one direct confrontation.

On a long straight stretch, with Lee at the wheel, they'd seen a panel truck driving fast toward them. The falling snow made it hard to see any details. Dave ordered Lee to get ready to accelerate and got the Skorpion ready. As they narrowed the gap, he climbed into the back of the Trackbreaker, changing places with Zera. He lowered his window a few inches and poked the muzzle of the machine pistol into the freezing air.

But the other vehicle didn't slow, moving at better than seventy miles per hour, swaying a little from side to side. Its windows were smoked glass, and the wipers were going full-out to keep the windshield clear.

"Should I stop, Dad?" asked Lee, leaning forward to try and see better.

"No." The road was slightly elevated, with a heavy wire fence close to its shoulder. If there was going to be trouble, there was no room to take any kind of evasive action.

But the other vehicle never slowed, barreling past with the snow whirling in the vortex of its passing. There was the taunting wail of its triple-note siren, and Dave glimpsed what might have been a gloved hand waving behind the shield.

Then it was gone, and Dave sighed with relief, remembering that only once had there been anything like a direct threat against them.

That had been earlier, when they were driving on one of the rare sunny afternoons. The road climbed the side of a mountain, zigging and zagging like a snake with a broken back. On one of the blind turns, Dave suddenly found himself facing a tangled mess of fallen branches. He braked immediately.

Lee reached for the door handle to get out of the passenger side, but Dave checked him.

"No. Could be a trap."

"Looked like an ordinary fall."

At that moment a large boulder came smashing down just in front of the hood, exploding into a thousand splinters of orange rock. Something thudded on the roof, making it ring. Zera had grabbed at the nearest weapon, Dave's 12-gauge Browning, looking around for some sight of their attackers.

"Above us," snapped Dave. Glancing in the rearview mirror, he was trying to work out his chances of reversing down the steep, winding highway. Every ten yards or so there was a stubby white post to mark the drop into the canyon.

Another large rock, ten feet in diameter, rolled across the road in front of the truck, vanishing over the edge into the abyss beyond. The jumble of wood ahead of them looked impenetrable, and if the Trackbreaker got stuck in there . . .

"Dad, let me. . . ."

Something pinged noisily off the roof. Dave hadn't much experience of being under fire, but he knew what a rifle bullet sounded like. He swore, putting the vehicle into the special manual-override reverse, letting up the pedal fast, hearing the screech of rubber.

Something banged against the side of the truck, snapping off the mirror and ripping off a section of the protective wire.

For about thirty seconds it was the most hair-raising thing that Dave Rand had ever done. With one mirror missing, he had to drive looking back over his shoulder, while Zera ducked out of his line of sight and Melmoth jumped up and down, barking with a furious excitement.

The rear wheels skidded on the edge, and twice he heard the crack of the warning posts vanishing behind him. On one of the crookback bends there was a sickening lurch as a wheel hung out in space for several heart-stopping moments, then found grip once more.

He was vaguely aware of the young woman pattering something that might have been a prayer while, at his side, his son just kept repeating "Dad, watch it, Dad, watch it, Dad!" in a high, breathless monotone.

There didn't seem to have been any more of the tumbled boulders, and he began to slow down, easing his foot onto the brake, knowing the risk of going off at the last moment on the loose stones and ice. Eventually the four-by came back under his control and slowed to something around a walk.

Then there was a turning place, and he was able to reverse into it, stopping a moment and then sliding the gearshift into automatic drive. He moved cautiously down the trail again, toward the valley bottom.

Lee sighed. "You know that old saying of Granddad's about being scared?"

"Getting a touch of the Hershies, you mean?" Dave grinned, aware of how fast his heart was beating and how slippery the wheel felt in his fingers.

Zera laughed in the back seat. "I know what he meant, guys. Know what he meant."

The detour around the roadblock had taken them an extra forty miles out of their way, and diminished their shrinking supplies of gas still further.

"GAS IS THE PRIORITY for us now," said Dave, checking the diminished contents of the trailer.

Most of the food was gone, but he felt confident that hunting would keep them going as long as they kept away from the towns and edged into the wilderness of the high country.

"How much left?" Zera asked, appearing at his shoulder, standing close against him. Dave felt the slightly pleasurable yet uncomfortable stirring that he'd noticed several times in the past few days—and nights.

"Tank's half-full, and we're down to the last five gallons of spare. Get us...let's see. Get us around another two hundred miles, top. Probably less."

The weather had become miserable. A chill norther kept blowing during the day, and most nights saw a clammy fog drifting from the mountains ahead of them. In places it dropped visibility below twenty yards. Melmoth had never seen fog before and clearly didn't think much of it. He would not venture out of sight of the truck or the fire, constantly turning his head to face the circling walls of damp whiteness as though he feared an army of invisible enemies.

Lee came to join them, rubbing his hands together against the cold. His father took a couple of steps away from the young woman, feeling as though the boy had caught him in some sexual indiscretion. He mentally reassured himself with the thought that he and Janine had, a year before the Hit, agreed that each of them could accept experiences outside marriage. Dave hadn't done it, and he knew his wife hadn't, either. At least, he thought she hadn't.

"About two hundred miles, Dad?"

"Yeah, give or take fifty."

"Have to look for some."

Zera smiled. "I thought we had been looking for gas," she said.

Dave sniffed, wiping a gloved fist across his mouth. "Sure. But there's looking, and then there's *looking*. See? So far we've been looking for gas. Now we're going to start *looking* for gas."

"Grand View."

Dave glanced over his shoulder, at where Lee was perusing the Rand McNally. "What was that again?" he asked.

"I said 'Grand View.' Name of a little place, next along on the map."

"Nice name," Zera said. She was in the passenger seat, her window down a couple of inches, letting in a flow of cool air.

Off to the right they could see a spectacular storm, with lightning splashing the dark clouds with silver lace. They could hear the sonorous thunder, even above the engine's throaty growl.

"Time for us to take a detour," Dave suggested. "Have to look for some isolated place where there might be some gas still untouched."

IT HAD PROBABLY been originally a line shack from a working cattle ranch. Over the years it had been altered and added to, and had obviously changed hands several times. It was hidden away at the end of an overgrown dirt road, dusted with light snow, surrounded by a grove of live oaks.

The name on the black mailbox was Hitchcock.

Dave pulled in front of the main house, stopping but keeping the engine running. They stared intently at the building, paying particular attention to the paths, checking for the marks of feet.

"Windows are unbroken," Lee noted. He'd taken the Nikon glasses from their leather case and was sweeping the area around with them. "No tracks. Looks untouched to me."

Once the engine was silent, they rolled down the windows, listening and looking, but finding nothing but stillness.

"Let Melmoth out," said Dave. "See if he reckons it's safe."

The pit bull was generally eager to be out in the fresh air. It jumped down, sniffing the afternoon, then walked confidently toward an outdoor lamp and pissed up it.

They all laughed at the demonstration of territorial confidence.

"Reckon I'll do the same," Lee said, stepping out of the truck, scattergun in hand. Dave followed him, also holding a shotgun, the Line-baugh snug at his hip, while Zera hefted the nickel-plated Ruger that belonged to Janine.

The place was quiet, with just a light breeze tugging at the empty branches of the trees. The house was sheltered from the wind, looking well preserved. A double garage stood on the left, with a range of trim outbuildings beyond.

"Looks possible," Dave said quietly.

"I'll go around the back and check," Lee offered eagerly.

"Fine. Zera . . ."

"Yeah?"

"Stay here. Watch the four-by. Get in and throw the locks if there's trouble. Sound the horn, and we'll come running."

Lee paused at the corner of the house, stooping and peering at the gravel. "Marks of dogs here," he called. "Better keep Melmoth with you, Zera."

Dave paused before approaching the front door; it was patterned glass with a wrought-iron ivy tree over it. He looked at the higher ground away to the north of the house. On the way, around noon, he'd spotted smoke rising from somewhere among the hills, and he wondered if anyone had been watching their approach to the Hitchcocks' place.

The door wasn't locked, and he pushed it open, sniffing the still, dulled air. He was positive that nobody had been in there for a very long time.

It looked as though the owners had abandoned it before the Big One.

Moments later Dave Rand found that he was wrong. The Hitchcocks were still there.

23

*"We Got It Comin'." Sukie Wolfff's vid-disc was
the all-chart Number One in the week of 12 January 2049.*

It's goin' to be night
At the end of the day,
We got it comin'.
I'm gonna miss the light
I got nothin' more to say,
We got it comin'.
We been dying of life
With our own livin' death.
We got it comin'.
You can cut with a knife
Or stifle our breath,
We got it comin'.
Gracious goodness! It's a great ball of fire,
And it's comin'.
Experts expect we're goin' to expire,

Cos it's comin',
Yeah it's comin',
We got it comin',
We got it comin'.

24

The house was decorated in a spare, western style. The ceilings were low, white painted, and Navaho rugs hung on several of the walls. Oil paintings of desert scenes were placed at neat intervals along the hall, past the open doors. At the far end Dave could see the entrance to the kitchen. There was a flight of open wooden stairs, dark stained.

He heard the sound of a latch rattling, followed by his son's voice. "You in there, Dad?"

"Yeah. Just going to have a look up the stairs. Check out the food and then call Zera in. Make sure the 4x4 is locked behind her."

The stairs creaked under his boots and he kept his index finger loose on the trigger of the Browning 245. His eyes came level with the landing, and he saw four doors. One, half-open, revealed a bath, in a dull shade of green. The other three were all closed.

Next to the bathroom, as he'd expected, was the john. On the walls of the landing Dave noticed several stuffed birds, staring glassy-eyed down at him. The third door opened onto what was obviously the guest room. A pair of twin beds with a geometrically folded duvet sitting crisply on top of each. A row of books was centered on a bureau, mostly English thriller writers, Dave observed.

The moment he turned the carved wooden handle and pushed open the last door, Dave Rand knew what he was going to find. The smell of the air was slightly different. Tainted with the elusive memory of an old sour sweetness.

The Hitchcocks lay side by side on the large master bed. She was on her back, knees slightly drawn up, head turned toward the man, whose left arm lay across the woman's chest. He was on his side, facing her.

They'd been dead for at least eighteen months.

In the dry, undisturbed air of the house, their bodies had decomposed gently. They eyes had gone first, withering in the hollow pockets of bone. The lips and the other soft tissues had gone next. It had been cold enough for there to be little actual rotting; the flesh had simply tightened and become dark and leathery. The fingers had curled in as sinews contracted. The nails had carried on growing for some time, as had the hair.

The man now had a short, straggling beard, though the silver-framed photo on the bedside table showed him clean shaven. She had been dark haired, but silver now showed, glittering palely among the roots, close to the skull. From the picture, Dave guessed they had probably been in their early fifties.

"Dad?" Lee's voice, echoing up the stairs, made him jump.

"Yeah? I'm fine."

"Anything up there?"

"Just the folks who used to live here."

The boy started up to the second floor. "They dead, are they?"

"Looks like they just lay down and fell asleep. They must have...ah, here it is." He stooped to pick up a small brown medicine bottle. The label had faded, but it bore the name Hitchcock, Patricia, and carried a long name of a chemical compound.

The bottle was empty.

Lee paused in the doorway. "Hey, it looks like they caught the last chopper out in a real quiet way," he said.

"Looks like it. Let's leave them be and go downstairs, shall we?"

"What's that?" pointing with the barrel of his gun.

"What?"

"Cassette player there." The little machine sat on the floor on the man's side of the bed. Lee walked round and knelt down, peering at it.

"Set on Record, Dad."

"Leave it."

"Dad . . . ?"

Dave hesitated. There was a terrible sense of invading privacy, yet he had to admit he also felt great curiosity to know what the tape held, what had been recorded in the last minutes of life. In a way, it was as though they would get to know something about these people whose house they'd invaded—almost like a courtesy, an introduction.

"All right. Quickly."

"How 'bout Zera?"

"Go get her, Lee. I'll wait here for you both. Only fair she hears it, too, whatever it is."

"What about Melmoth?"

"Keep him out of the house, for the time being. Tie his lead round a tree."

While he waited, Dave looked out of the window, across the tops of the trees to the hills beyond. There was already some mist beginning to attach itself to the peaks, hanging there like fragments of torn shrouds. There was a narrow path winding down the side of the nearest hill, about a half a mile away. For a moment Dave thought he'd seen someone moving on the trail, but the fog came swirling down and he couldn't be certain. He remembered the smoke they'd seen earlier, and he decided that they might keep a watch during the night. It was just possible that someone might have spotted them driving up toward the isolated Hitchcock house.

"Oh, God!" Zera's soft voice expressed her shock as she came into the bedroom.

"They won't hurt us," said Dave, picking up the cassette player, pressing Rewind. He waited until it clicked off at the start of the tape then pressed Play, and waited.

There was a period of silence, and Dave looked at the spools, wondering if the batteries had run down. But the tape was moving from left to right. A faint hissing sound came next, and then someone coughing.

"I don't truly know why I'm doing this recording." The voice was calm, middle-aged, with a hint of a Southern accent. "A wish to leave something of a footprint in the sands of time, perhaps. My name is...soon it will be 'was'... Norman Hitchcock. My wife, Pat, and I have lived here for ten years. Moved from near New Orleans when I got bought out. My company made . . . well, that doesn't much matter. Nothing much matters now. Pat's gone before me, like we agreed. In case anything went wrong.''

Next they heard a clinking of glass and someone swallowing. ''There. That's the last of them. Helps to have a son who's a doctor. Gave us these a week ago, when it was obvious we were all in for it. Warned us to take the travel pills to stave off the nausea. Risk of bringing up the pills and puking.''

There was a period of silence on the tape. Lee was standing by the window, his back to the room. Zera leaned against the wall near the door. Dave stood by the bed, holding the machine, aware of its faint vibration, like the life of a tiny humming creature.

''Feel the muzziness. Pat said that. Way she went, it didn't seem too bad. No pain. No pain, no gain. Where did I . . . Starting to wander, aren't I? Won't be long, my dearest, and we'll . . . Said she'd wait for me, first turn in the road.''

The voice was beginning to hesitate, slurring the ends off some of the words. There were pauses, growing longer.

"If anyone ever listens t' this...Maybe there are survivors, but we were running low on food an'...saved for a good last meal...las' supper... Gotta lie down by my love...only love...Mustn't fall down an'... Together for ever...like we lived so we...This is Norman Hitchcock signin' off...Seems a pity...can't talk anymore...'s'all, folks..."

The tape ran on in whispering silence until Dave pressed the Stop button with a decisive, loud click. He carefully laid the machine down where they'd found it, caught the eyes of Zera and Lee and gestured in the direction of the door.

He followed them out onto the landing, closing the door firmly behind him.

"Let's go downstairs," he said.

It was what Dave had hoped. Isolated properties, well off main highways, were likely to be a good bet for supplies. The disaster of January 2049 had struck so quickly and had proved so impossible to combat that the death toll had been truly catastrophic. Apart from the first wave of slaughter, the second phase of dying had come swiftly, not giving a chance for the people running from the megadeath cities to reach places like the Hitchcock home.

There was little food left in the cupboards. A few packets of soup and some cake mixes. Three bottles of designer water and some tins of prunes. Nearly thirty tins of prunes.

"Could help to pass the time," said Zera, grinning.

But the best news was the gasoline. There were a couple of five-gallon cans, as well as a large drum, over half-full, that still held around twenty gallons.

"Load up the four-by, Lee," said Dave. "Should be enough to get us up to Montana. Then . . . we'll have to see how things turn."

By now the fog had thickened, reducing visibility to a scant fifty yards. The outbuildings were simply ghostly outlines, and the stark shapes of the trees were etched against the shifting whiteness. Melmoth was becoming more and more unhappy and trailed the heels of whoever was nearest to the house. Twice he stopped and bellied down in the gravel of the driveway, whining his discomfort.

Evening was also closing in. Dave kept thinking about the shadowy figures that he thought he'd seen. But he could have been wrong, haunted by the need for wariness as he was.

Once the vehicle was filled up, he got his son to drive it to the back of the main house, parking it very close to the rear entrance. He also checked the doors and windows of the house, locking some storm shutters in place over the most vulnerable ones.

Zera had come to help him, standing close as she struggled with the damp-swollen locks. "Think there's going to be trouble, Dave?"

"Could be. We'll sleep shifts tonight. Take three hours on and six hours off."

The young woman put a hand on his arm. "I don't think I'd ever be frightened of anything with you around, Dave."

He laughed and patted her hand, moving away when he suddenly noticed that Lee had entered the room. Zera smiled at the boy and walked off toward the kitchen. "I'll make us some coffee," she said.

Lee looked at his father. Lifting his voice into a plaintive falsetto, he fluted, "Oh, gee, Dave . . . I don't think I'll ever be scared of anything with you here to protect me."

To his great embarrassment, Zera had come back in behind him. "Yeah, I saw that old movie once, so lay off, you little nerd!"

Dave had never seen his son blush so deeply since the school sports day ten years earlier, when he'd suffered a disastrous accident to his shorts while leading the sixty yards dash.

Nothing more was said on the subject, and anyway, the night was upon them.

Lee insisted on taking first watch, running from ten until one in the morning. They'd brought the firearms in from the Trackbreaker, and the lad had decorated himself with two pistols and the SIG-Sauer 120 Lux across his shoulder. The Onyx was ready on a table on the second-floor landing.

"Where're you sleeping, Dad? In the guest room? Or on the sofa downstairs?"

Dave stared hard at his son, suspecting that something lay behind the question. But Lee met his gaze with an open smile.

"Sofa. Zera can have the bed upstairs."

"Oh, that's ridiculous, Dave. Two perfectly good beds! What's wrong?"

"Nothing. Just that . . ."

The young woman shook her head, the bright blue eyes piercing the gloom of the living room. "You don't think I'm going to try and seduce you, do you? You really...you flatter yourself, Mr. Rand. I don't go for old men."

So he took the bed nearest the door, and Zera the one by the window. He simply slipped off his boots and jeans, while she also kicked off her boots and peeled off the jeans, leaving her in a plain green T-shirt and pale blue bikini pants.

Lee checked in, making sure that they all had the same time on their watches. "Any problem, and I'll wake you both," he said. "I'll keep Melmoth around with me."

"How's the fog?"

"Real thick. Just about see the four-by from the kitchen window." He went out, closing the door quietly behind him, the light from one of the torches they'd found in the garage flickering away down the stairs.

"You sure you don't want me to take the next lookout?" whispered Zera.

"No. Thanks, but I'll do it. Old man like me doesn't need as much sleep as you young folk."

She giggled, invisible in the blackness. Dave pulled the duvet over him and was quickly asleep.

He blinked awake, feeling someone moving the bedclothes off him, then replacing them. "What's . . . ? Time already, Lee?"

He felt the hand caressing his chest, then a soft body pressed against his. "Move over, old man," she said.

25

Edited extracts from a CBS live special, reporting on the attempt by combined forces from both the Western and Eastern blocs to destroy the approaching asteroid by the use of missiles. Dated 8 January 2049.

"I guess everyone's seen and heard enough in the last few days about how this venture is going to work ... so I'll just repeat, for any hermits who haven't been watching or listening, that this is *the* day.

"From the remnants of President Reagan's Star Wars system, enhanced during those golden days of President Quayle's two terms, we have the finest, diamond-best rockets the world has ever seen. An array of those, combined with other missiles from every part of the world, are aimed right at the rocky heart of Adastreia. The countdown is running, and there's fifty-five seconds to blast-off.

"It'll be several hours before we know whether or not the operation has been successful. Not that the experts from both sides have any doubts. Gregori Kosintzev from the Lake Baikal base has promised us one-hundred-percent victory. Nothing bigger than a baby's thumbnail will enter our atmosphere, Gregori claims.

"Six, five, preignition under way, two, one and blast-off! And all our prayers go with these dozens of sleek monsters as they rise serenely into the winter sky."

Excerpt, the following day.

"There they go! God, it's so beautiful! Through the big-screen image enhancer we can all see hit after hit after hit. Chunks of the asteroid are vanishing into deepest space. Yes, it's official! The Earth is *saved!*

26

Dave glanced at his watch. Outside the window the clouds had drifted away, and there was an unusually bright moon, struggling through the dense fog. He could see his breath in the cold bedroom.

It was just after midnight.

He yawned and raised himself on one elbow, looking down at the face of the young woman sleeping beside him. The silver light heightened the planes of her cheeks, making them harsher. She wasn't what Dave would have called pretty. Definitely not that. But it was a very good face. Honest, he thought, leaning and brushing away an errant curl of blond hair from over the eyes. Since traveling with them, Zera hadn't bothered to cut it, and it was now growing out nicely. Dave preferred it longer.

She woke at the touch and grinned up at him, showing her perfect, white teeth. "Morning, old man," she said, pulling his head down to her and kissing him fiercely on the lips, the tip of her tongue probing hotly into his mouth.

"Morning, young lady," he replied, breaking away from her and, surprised at his own instant response, wanting to make love to her again. But he couldn't forget that Lee's stint on watch was coming to an end.

Her hand was already reaching for him, but he wriggled agilely away, sitting up on the edge of the bed. Both of them had quickly shed the rest of their clothes, taking pleasure in each other's nakedness. Now the cold hit him, and Dave shivered.

"Ghost walking over your grave?" she asked him, also sitting up. The duvet fell below her breasts and he stared at them, the nipples hardened in the pale air.

"What? Oh, no. No. Just thought I'd better get up."

"Looks like you're already..." she began, stopping when they both heard the faint echo of footsteps out in the corridor.

"I'll get dressed. You go back to sleep. I'll wake you when it's time for your turn."

He rummaged down the bed for his thermal vest, then pulled it on. As he stood up, he was suddenly aware of the almost pristine condition of the second twin bed. He swore under his breath, walking quickly across and messing up the pillows and duvet. Wryly he shook his head at the deceit he was already being sucked into.

Zera had pulled the covers up over her, watching him dress. "You feel bad about this, Dave?" she asked.

"No. No, I don't."

"Will you tell your wife?"

"I don't know," he said, realizing with some surprise that this was a totally honest response. "I don't even know if I'll ever see Janine again, anyway."

"Yeah," she said flatly, turning away from him.

They didn't really need such emotional problems, Dave thought and shrugged in resignation. None of them knew anything about the future, so why should they start getting all twisted up inside? A day at a time, he told himself. A day at a time.

He decided not to finish getting dressed until he'd had a quick wash. They'd found water in the head tank in the house, even thought it was bitingly cold. Dave couldn't be bothered with heating it up on one of their small camping stoves.

He winced at the chill of the water on his groin. As he soaped himself, he again heard Lee walk softly by, keeping up his patrol around the house. Dave licked his lips, aware that he could taste Zera on his tongue. Somehow the thought of using one of the toothbrushes in the dusty tumbler on the bathroom shelf didn't appeal to him. He squeezed paste on his index finger and rubbed it around his mouth, then rinsed it out into the basin.

When he'd finishing getting dressed, he buckled on the Linebaugh. Pausing in the bedroom, he looked down at the girl's figure.

"Zera?" he said very quietly.

"Yeah," she responded instantly.

Dave leaned over the bed and touched her on the back of the neck. "Just wanted to say that . . . well, it's all right. You know?"

"Sure. I know," she said, and squeezed his fingers.

He got downstairs to find Lee tired looking but alert. He hadn't seen or heard anything during his spell on watch. "Fog's so thick it's hard," he said. "Could be an army of crazed zombies lurking out there."

Dave smiled. "Thanks, son. With that haunted and morbid thought, I'll leave you to go off to bed."

"Sure. Oh, Melmoth doesn't seem happy."

"Might be the fog?"

Lee shrugged. "Could be. But it was kind of creepy. He kept sort of snarling and trying to get up someplace so he could see out one of the windows.''

The pit bull was in the hall with them, its head turning from side to side. Dave noticed that the short hairs along its spine were bristling.

"Go to bed, but don't get undressed. Just in case you need to come running."

"G'night, Dad."

"Sleep well, son. Nice dreams." Only after the lad had gone up the stairs did Dave realize that he hadn't said "nice dreams" to Lee for about ten years.

The house was Dave's to look after, and he admired how well Lee had handled being alone. He was going to mature more quickly, Dave thought as he went through a weapons check.

He had the big handgun on his belt, with the Browning slung across his shoulder. The Skorpion had been on the table in the living room. But on his second tour of the house, he began to feel distinctly uncomfortable and picked it up.

"You can feel something, can't you, boy?" he said, stooping to pat Melmoth. The dog rubbed itself against his legs, mouth half-open, panting as if it had been for a run.

Man and animal both heard it at the very same moment. A far-off howling. A long, keening sound that made Melmoth quiver and begin to snarl. Dave turned toward the source of the banshee wail, somewhere off to the west of them.

"Big pack of dogs," he said, partly to reassure himself with the noise of his own voice. "Lee said he'd seen some tracks. Don't worry, Melmoth. They can't get at us in here. Sounds like they're a good five miles away."

But the pit bull didn't seem content with mere words. It left Dave and walked stiff legged into the small study that opened off the end of the hall near the kitchen. Dave followed the animal. The room was only about twelve feet square, with a large desk at its center and shelves of books. The window was covered with a heavy venetian blind, the slats closed. It was one of the rooms that had big storm shutters over the outside of the casement.

Melmoth had stopped and was glaring at the window, snarling deep in its chest. Its hackles were raised, and there was a thread of saliva trickling from the open jaws. Dave cocked the machine pistol and carefully reached with cold fingers to set the selector to full-auto.

With his left hand he grasped the cord that opened the blinds and tugged on it. There was a microsecond of recognition and bewilderment that the outside shutters were open, letting the mist-filtered moonlight into the room.

Melmoth started to bark furiously. Dave stared into the blank rectangle of fog, trying to see what was there . . .

The face, bearded and red eyed, loomed from the whiteness. Hands smashed the glass and grabbed for his throat. In his shock, Dave dropped the Skorpion to the carpet.

He opened his mouth to yell for help, but the fingers were like steel claws, choking him into lifeless silence.

27

The United States Department of Civil Defense. A public announcement on 9 January 2049.

You will all be aware that the attempt yesterday to destroy the rogue asteroid, Adastreia, by the use of missiles from many countries has not been the success that we all hoped.

Some damage is reported from space agencies all over the world, but it has not proved sufficient to check its momentum and progress toward our planet.

It now seems quite likely that some parts of the asteroid may strike Earth. But our experts are certain that most of it will be destroyed as it burns up through our atmosphere. There is a possibility of some residual damage from the pieces of rock that might remain.

Impact now looks like being some time on 12 January, but it is not feasible to point to any particular area as being under special threat.

However, there are some basic precautions that we can all take. And if any of you have neighbors who are elderly or infirm, do what you can to help and reassure them.

Keep a television on, tuned to a news channel at least once an hour. There will be constant updates on the potential risk. You will be able to know if your region is a likely zone several hours before impact time.

If there is no risk, then you need take no precautions. Otherwise, simply place tape over your windows and leave doors open to allow any blast to pass clean on through. Turn off and unplug electrical appliances. There is no need whatsoever to buy stocks of food or drink. There will positively be no shortages.

If you require any further information, call the toll-free number now showing on the bottom of your screen.

Remember that there is no cause for concern or alarm. The threat is small, and the risks almost nonexistent.

28

Dave Rand knew he was dying.

Never in his life had he encountered even a fraction of the muscular power that was throttling him. He scrabbled at the man's wrists, trying to grab a finger and bend it back. But the grip was too tight, and he could feel consciousness slipping away from him. There was the vague awareness of blood trickling down his throat as the attacker's nails drove into his flesh.

The jagged splinters of glass in the window frame snapped out as he struggled, trying to break free.

"Eey-aayee..." The shriek tumbled from bared teeth in the fog-haloed face.

Sound was fading, and Melmoth's furious barking was falling away as though it was being enveloped in thick wool. Dave's hands slipped off the thick, strong wrists, and he started to slump. Something brushed against his fingers. Cold. Rough and hard. Like the hilt of a knife.

It was willpower alone that helped him to draw the Trail-Master from its sheath, hacking upward with the razored ten-inch steel blade and feeling it slice into the man's wrist.

Blood spurted immediately, and the grip loosened, enabling Dave to suck in a wheezing breath. A faint surge of his own strength coursed back, powering his will to fight and survive.

"Lee! Lee! Lee!" he yelled, cutting at the attacker's other hand, slicing one of the fingers clear off, leaving a raw stump that jetted dark blood into the room.

Free, he staggered several paces backward, sheathing the blood-slick knife and fumbling for the Skorpion. The bearded man had vanished with a howl of fury and pain, leaving ragged shreds of his parka on the shards of broken glass. From out in the fog there was shouting and then the crack of a hunting rifle. A bullet broke one of the top panes of the window and buried itself in the wall a yard from where Dave was crouching.

He scrambled toward the broken window, where tendrils of freezing fog were already drifting in, and flattened himself against the wall. Pointing the muzzle of the machine pistol outside, he triggered a quick burst. Eight of the twenty rounds of full-metal-jacket 9 mm bullets racketed out into the night. Dave didn't expect to actually hit anyone, but he figured that the attackers wouldn't relish coming against automatic fire.

Melmoth spun around and went at top speed out of the study and along the hall, heading for the other end of the house. Dave swallowed painfully and decided to follow the pit bull. As he passed the bottom of the stairs, he glimpsed Lee and Zera out of the corner of his eye, at the top of the landing.

"Take front and back and stay in cover!" he called. "Don't know how many."

"You all right?" He heard Zera's question vanishing into the darkness behind him. Dave was hot on the heels of the barking and there was no time to reply.

The shutters on the other end room had also been torn open, and there was a dark figure, looming halfway in through the window. Before Dave could take a shot, Melmoth struck.

The invader had one leg down on the floor, and the dog hit it like an antitank missile. Dave clearly heard the dry crack of a bone breaking above the sound of the man beginning to scream. Melmoth was in his element. The bank of white fog outside had disturbed him, and then there'd been the howling of the pack of running dogs. Now this was something that he could understand and react to.

The man had been holding a shotgun, its stock wrapped in baling wire, but he dropped that outside the window, leaning backward as he tried to get away from the dog. But that just gave the pit bull an easier target for its raging aggression.

The animal climbed the outstretched leg, hauling itself up with teeth and claws, higher, above the knees. Quickly reaching the tender, soft flesh of the groin.

There was the muffled boom of the Onyx from up the stairs, and a yelp of pain. Dave glanced once more at Melmoth, seeing that the dog was virtually out of the window, jaws still locked tight on the attacker. There was nothing for him to do there, so he turned and went back into the hall, near the front door.

Everything seemed to be happening at once.

He heard Zera's voice, high and thin with anger and fear, and then the light snap of the nickel-plated Ruger. There was a thunderous crash against the front door and a sheet of flame lit up the front of the house. Dave suddenly feared for their car and sprinted through into the kitchen, lifting a corner of the blind and peering out. He could just see the squat shape of the truck. There didn't seem to be anyone out there.

Taking a chance, he turned the key in the dead-lock, eased the door open and slipped into the cold whiteness.

The freezing air stabbed at him, irritating his damaged throat, making him want to cough. He stood still, getting his bearings. Through all the brawling he'd kept the scattergun and he unslung it, replacing it on his shoulder with the half-empty Skorpion. There was a momentary temptation to try and dig out one of the spare mags from the trailer, but he resisted it. From all the chaos he could hear, time was running out faster than sand from a broken hourglass.

The fog was as thick as anything he'd ever seen, making it tough to see more than six feet in any direction. He began to circle back to the front of the house, almost immediately tripping over something. He bent down, groping along the ground, his hand touching the stickiness of warm blood. Dave leaned forward, making out the bearded corpse, seeing the black hole drilled through the center of the forehead, and another patch of blood in the middle of the chest. Zera making good use of Janine's .32 Ruger.

There was the sound of feet on gravel, pounding toward him, and Dave readied the Browning. He experienced a moment of doubt that it might be Lee, then he heard his son's voice, shouting somewhere above him.

A shadowy form loomed ahead. The shotgun kicked against his shoulder, and the stranger vanished as if some master puppeteer had tugged at its strings. There was a scrabbling sound and a low, bubbling moaning, and then no more noise.

"Dad! Where are you?"

Dave decided not to risk answering. Clearly there were other members of the attacking gang, and any of them could be standing within ten feet of him. He picked his way carefully around to the front of the house and saw the pile of burning wood against the main floor. The fire had cleared away the worst of the fog, and he could make out a group of figures. Five men, all wrapped in heavy furs.

A couple had pump-action shotguns, and each and every one was armed with pistols. Dave didn't hesitate. If any of them turned and saw him, he was a goner. He leveled the machine pistol and squeezed the trigger.

The last twelve rounds sprayed the group, knocking four of them to the gravel. The Skorpion hit the dirt, and Dave fired off the Browning, putting down the fifth member of the gang.

Spinning on his heel, Dave ran back around the building, vaulting the corpse, and reentered through the kitchen door.

Facing him was the spectral apparition of Melmoth. The pit bull blocked the hall from Dave, foursquare and immovable, teeth bared, muzzle streaked with blood. Tattered fragments of God knows what flesh hung from the jaws.

If it were possible for a dog to smile, then Melmoth was smiling.

"Good boy," Dave said hoarsely. "Let's go see if we can find us some more of the bastards and snuff 'em."

He led the pit bull into the shadowy hall. The fire outside the main door seemed to be dying down a little, though smoke curled and lurked in the darker corners. Dave stopped at the bottom of the stairs and peered upward.

"Lee! Zera?"

Two faces appeared over the rounded oak balustrade that ran around the top landing.

"You all right?"

"Sure. I reckon I took out at least two of them with the Onyx."

"Good boy."

"And I think I hit one with the Ruger," Zera said.

"You did. His body's out back of the house, just around the corner. Any sign of them coming at us again?"

"Fog's too thick," replied Lee. "How many did you take out, Dad? Heard the Skorpion. And also I heard Melmoth."

"Between the four of us, I reckon we've accounted for at least five dead and some others that won't be feeling too great in the morning."

Outside there was a yell, and a ragged volley of four or five shots was fired blindly at the building, breaking a couple more windows.

"Here they come!" Dave shouted, even as he sprinted in a semicrouch to the living room, ready to try and repel any further attack.

But that had been the last angry and futile gesture from the assaulting gang. Dave, Lee and Zera stayed awake and on guard for the rest of the night, but there was no sign of any further attack. At least not by half-mad humans.

The dogs came around two-fifteen in the morning, with the weather deteriorating. By one o'clock a blizzard had started raging in earnest, the snow beating through the mist. After about an hour the window had eased, and the snowfall had abated. But the dense mist closed in again.

Melmoth heard the pack first. Lee had taken the animal into the bathroom and managed to clean off most of the blood. Just as he'd finished, the hackles of the pit bull went up again and he began to snarl.

"Dad," Lee called urgently.

Dave was on the stairs, and he came up immediately. "What is it?"

"Melmoth. He's heard something. Must be those men back again."

"Quiet. Listen."

Then they could all hear it. Closer and louder, carrying through the fog. The cry of a pack of wild hunting dogs.

It was moonfall, and the light outside was vanishing fast.

Melmoth was becoming more and more excited and started to stalk up and down the first floor, giving out short, angry barks. Dave watched the dog and finally decided something must be done.

"If those other dogs hear him, they might try and get in. With the shutters broken down and some of the windows gone, we're vulnerable. We could get into one of the top rooms and lock the door. They'd never break in, but I'd rather they didn't even try."

For a moment the house rocked gently as a tremor shook the surrounding hills. Glass and china tinkled, and a small section of the wall cracked, showering plaster on the floor. Outside, the howling of the approaching dogs redoubled in volume.

Dave knelt and called Melmoth to him. He stroked the heavy shoulders and the thrusting muzzle, trying to soothe the animal. "Come on, boy. Calm down, boy, calm down." Gradually he felt the adrenaline rush of tension easing from himself and the quietness communicating itself to the pit bull. The snarling slowed down and finally stopped.

"To be on the safe side, let's go up and keep watch from the top floor," said Dave, and led the way.

They were exhausted, and it seemed as though dawn would never struggle through the fog.

Dave's throat was swollen, and he was finding it difficult to swallow. He'd drunk several glasses of the icy water to try and ease it. He was in the bathroom, with Lee keeping him company, when Zera called to them.

"Almighty... Hey, come here."

There was no suggestion of imminent danger in her voice, and the father and son took their time to join her in the guest room, which overlooked the path around the house. The fog was finally slinking back to its mountain retreat.

"Look. The dogs were busy."

"Oh, Christ! That's horrible." Dave closed his eyes and turned away.

"Guess they were dead anyway," offered Lee. "But it's double gross-out."

Judging by the mangled remains, the dogs *had* been busy.

Considering that there must have been close on a dozen armed men attacking the house, Dave realized that they'd been lucky. If the gang had known they were fairly well prepared, they could have come at it differently. The result would have been lethal.

Five corpses were scattered about on the grounds. All of them had been attacked and partly devoured by the invisible pack of dogs in the night. Since the faces were the most exposed, it had been there that the animals had wrought their best work. It was a bizarre sight: the five bodies, warmly dressed in windbreakers and parkas, but with only gnawed skulls, eyeless, featureless, protruding into the morning chill.

One had also been emasculated, lying in a great lake of congealed blood, just outside a first-floor window. Dave noted that one of the trio of bodies near the front of the house, cut down by the burst from the Skorpion, was missing a finger, newly severed. So he'd gotten his attacker.

THEY PACKED the Trackbreaker quickly and quietly, hurried by the stench of death around them. Zera picked up an old Smith & Wesson M3000 12-gauge—the folding butt version—and stashed it on the back seat of the four-by.

Dave was self-conscious with her, not knowing how the young woman wanted to play the change in their relationship. But she seemed oblivious to the previous night's lovemaking, and his own feeling of tension gradually eased.

Melmoth was subdued, eager to jump into the tailgate space and lie down patiently and wait for them to hit the road again. Lee looked pale and drawn, still in a state of numb shock from the attack and the butchery of the dark, foggy hours.

Dave got behind the wheel, looking out through the grilled shield, seeing the toppling thunderheads away to the east that warned of a massive storm on the ride. There was also the bitter taste of ash hanging in the air, slightly sulphurous. Somewhere, perhaps five hundred miles away, there had been one of the almost ceaseless eruptions that had become commonplace since the Big Hit had rocked the seismic clock.

But away to the north the sky looked a little clearer.

29

Their plan to cut cross-country in the neighborhood of Yellowstone Park was frustrated.

Dave was asleep in the back seat, with Zera dozing in the front, when they were both woken by the 4x4 slowing to a halt. Lee put on the hand brake.

"Sorry, folks. Looks like we've lost out here. Sign there says all highways east of Idaho Falls toward Wyoming are closed. Have to try and go north toward Butte."

Even that route was difficult. As they neared the site of the Idaho Atomic Energy Commission plant, the road simply vanished. It stopped under a massive mountain of reddish earth, overlaid with gray, glasslike dust.

Dave took over the wheel and he didn't delay, reversing carefully and moving fast in the opposite direction until he could pick a trail that would still lead them the right way.

"What do you think happened there?" asked Zera, turning in the front to stare back. "It looked double weird."

Dave peered into his rearview mirror. "God only knows. Looks like there was some kind of awful explosion or something."

Lee was staring out of the passenger's window. "You noticed that all the plants are dead. Kind of shriveled and shrunk, and there's not a sign of a bird for miles."

It was a bleak and depressing place, and Dave was glad when they got far enough away to be able to camp for the night.

They rolled on, slowly and as it sometimes seemed, endlessly. Two nights later, after some of the toughest off-road driving they'd encountered, they were deep into Montana.

Granny Bronsky, Janine's mother, lived far north in the mountain wilderness, close by Glacier Park. East of Kalispell, between the Swan and Flathead ranges. If the gods had been kind, then there was every reason to think that they might have survived the initial cataclysm of Adastreia's impact on Earth.

Dave had picked as quiet a spot as he could for their camp. Coming off a highway treacherous with sheet ice, he drove along a narrow dirt road that wound itself right beneath the road through a cramped tunnel. It was dry and out of the wind.

A stream flowed down past them, bone-chillingly cold. Lee set up the stove while Dave made a check on their supplies. They had enough gas, but the food was running very low. Over the past day or so he'd considered whether they could stop and sidetrack for a hunting trip. But now he was so close to his wife and daughters, he didn't want any further delay.

His encounter with Zera still kept rising in his mind on a tide of blood. But neither of them had mentioned it again, though the young woman had several times touched his arm lightly, and once stroked his stubbled cheek with gentle fingertips. Dave didn't know what to think about it, and decided that the easiest thing to do was nothing.

They hadn't seen any sign of human life for three days, and Dave didn't think it was necessary to post any kind of watch. But it was a bitingly cold night, dropping at least twenty below. Despite Dave's reservations, Zera insisted on taking her turn at sleeping out. Lee took the front seat and his father the back. There was enough room in the depleted trailer for the young woman to get under the tarp with her sleeping bag.

Dave's worry was that there might be grizzly around, but a search of the area right up to the overhead highway hadn't revealed the spoors of anything bigger than a beaver.

Melmoth woke them just after midnight. It had begun to snow quite hard, but the wind had dropped. The veil of whiteness fell straight down, like a theater curtain. Dave opened his eyes, shushing the pit bull's deep-throated snarling. Lee also came awake, sitting up and trying to look out.

"Can't see anything, Dad. Want me to get out and check?"

"No. We'll both get out and take a look. Pull your weatherproof on. Way past freezing out there, and I don't want to run the engine for heating."

It took a couple of minutes to get their warm clothing on, ease out of the truck and quickly close the doors behind them to trap whatever heat might linger. Dave quieted the dog and kept him inside. Bear was a possibility, and he didn't trust Melmoth not to fancy its chances against a thousand-pound grizzly.

But it wasn't bear. It was horses. Now they were out in the open, in the steady snowfall, they could both clearly hear the clopping sound of hooves on the highway nearby.

Father and son looked at each other.

"Wake Zera?" whispered Lee.

Dave nodded his agreement. It sounded like a really large party, twenty or thirty animals, going by the noise. And nothing much had happened since the Hit to make Dave want to rely on the warmth and generosity of his fellow man. "I'll get the Skorpion. Wake her fast and quiet. Then we'll keep under cover. Hope they don't see us."

The woman hefted the Smith & Wesson scattergun, while Lee had both his Onyx and the 9mm SIG-Sauer. Dave had the machine pistol, the shotgun and the Linebaugh.

Zera and Lee hid under the overhang, while Dave went to the farther side of the clearing, behind the snow-covered four-by. From there he could just see part of the highway, behind a stone wall, through a thicket of ponderosa pines.

It was the biggest group of people he'd seen in over twenty months. All well wrapped in thick clothes, making it impossible to tell if they were male or female. The leaders were certainly male, singing together as they heeled their horses on through the snow. A repetitive chorus from a big hit from a gyrating, loin-thrusting long-hair group.

"I'm gonna make you want what I want you to want, foxy." The last word was bellowed out with raucous laughter.

Dave concentrated on remaining hidden while he tried a head-count and cataloging what kind of armaments they carried. It was an impressive array of weaponry. Virtually everyone wore rifles over their shoulders, and a couple had light machine guns. Because of the steady veil of whiteness, Dave couldn't make out any details like caliber or manufacturer. There were also a half-dozen mules, loaded with supplies.

For a moment, above the noise of the singing and the clatter of the hooves on the rutted ice, Dave thought he heard a female voice crying out— a woman or a young girl. Then there was the sound of a slap and a muffled sob. Whoever rode with the gang didn't sound much like she was enjoying it.

A very tall man brought up the rear. Riding a milk white stallion, he sat head and shoulders above the others. Despite the cold and the snow, he rode bareheaded, revealing a tumbling mane of blond hair—hair so light in color that it looked almost white. He seemed to be scouting the area, turning from side to side as he rode. He reined in his mount when he was level with Dave, and even at that distance, knowing he was invisible, Dave felt the need to shrink back into deeper cover. But at the last second he resisted the urge, understanding that any movement might make him stand out like a salmon in a bathtub.

The man coughed and spit in a wide arc. Slapping his horse on the flank with a gloved hand, he made the animal surge forward. Only when the sound had faded away into the forest stillness, did Dave relax. His throat felt tight, his lungs too full, and he realized he'd been holding his breath for an unnaturally long time.

THE NEXT AFTERNOON SAW them close to their destination. On the way they saw evidence that confirmed that Dave had done the right thing by keeping out of sight while the horsemen passed by. It was a couple of hours after what would have been sunup on a normal day, and Lee was driving with the window down when he smelled smoke.

"Up ahead. Drifting across the highway. Looks like a house on fire."

"Keep moving. Could be a trap."

Once they were past, it was clear it wasn't a trap. But it looked like the ferocious handiwork of the blond giant and his horsemen.

They looked on in silence as Lee kept the truck moving steadily. The building—or what remained of it—showed signs of having been fortified. There were bars over the remaining windows, and a plate of steel had been hammered over the broken door. But it hadn't saved the occupants.

The drifting smoke was acrid, and Dave cranked up his window to close it out. But that didn't close out the sight of the four mangled, tortured corpses.

"How can any human do that to other human beings?" Zera asked in horror.

"Reckon it might have been there all along. Look back at history. Religious massacres. Holocaust. The beast's there in everyone. Just waiting for the right time and place." Dave shook his head. "And apparently some can't resist it."

It wasn't just the fact that four people had been slaughtered. It was the obvious gloating pleasure that had been taken in the deed. The care with which the body of the young boy had been crucified, upside down over a smoldering fire, demonstrated that well enough.

Dave hoped that the death-dealing wound of the crimson gash that gaped below the chin had been inflicted very quickly and very early.

IN THE LAST FEW MILES to Granny Bronsky's house there was dramatic evidence of serious earthquake activity. The highway buckled and tipped like a swaybacked mule, making their progress slower than ever. It took more than an hour to cover the final mile and a half. Dave took the wheel, carefully steering the vehicle in its lowest gear. The weather was a little warmer, pushing the temperature above freezing and turning the frozen earth into slippery ruts of unforgiving mud.

"Lot of horse tracks," observed Zera.

"Only way of getting around," Dave commented.

And then they were there. The first glance of the neat frame house was from a rise in the dirt road, about a quarter-mile off.

"Looks all right," Lee said as Dave braked. "Can't see anyone around, though."

The mailbox saying Bronsky was knocked off its pedestal, peppered with bullet holes. Dave leaned on the wheel, overwhelmed with a sudden chilling desolation. Things were very wrong.

The truck sighed to a halt in the front yard, and all three of them got out, followed by a subdued Melmoth. For several long heartbeats none of them spoke. It was Lee who broke the silence.

"It's wrecked," he said in a faltering voice.

Even from the outside it was obvious that Granny's home had been devastated. Drapes were torn, and the front door stood swinging, half off its hinges. A couple of windows were smashed, and broken bottles littered what was once a trim vegetable garden at the side.

There was a deadly stillness and emptiness. Nothing, nobody stirred in the desolate ruins.

Cans of paint had been emptied over the white-painted walls, and there was obscene graffiti everywhere. It looked as though a horde of malicious children had run riot.

"Shall we go in?" Lee asked.

"In a minute. No hurry. Janine and the girls aren't here."

"But we have to find out if they were at some point. Must be clues inside."

The house had once been part of a working farm, and the old corral still stood to the left, next to a large Dutch barn. Dave looked at it for a long minute, seeing the clearest evidence that a number of horses had been kept there recently.

"You two stay here. I'm going around the back. Just take a quick look."

His boots splashed in the mud as he walked away, past the open doors of the empty garage. He felt as though someone had drilled a bottomless well clear into his guts. After the long period when he was certain that Janine, Ellie and Roxie were dead, there had come the time-traveling postcard, bringing with it a new flickering hope. A flicker that had been growing stronger with every mile they covered toward Montana. But he felt a renewed sense of dread.

He saw the fresh grave as soon as he turned the corner. The rear prospect of the house was toward the snow-covered mountains of the north. Once there had been a lawn and a garden swing; now there was only trampled desolation, fringed with scrubby bushes.

And a fresh-dug grave.

He stopped, stricken, not wanting to move another step forward at the sight of a jagged-edged cupboard door stuck into a mound of raw earth. With lettering, black and sharp, on it.

Dave closed his eyes for a few moments, gathering strength to himself. Then he took the few steps necessary to bring him close enough to read the words above the grave: "Janine Rand, daughter, wife and mother. Murdered here. September 2050. Pray for her."

Dave stared at the reddish clay beneath his boots. "The girls?" he said, not even aware he'd spoken out loud.

"Gone," said a quiet voice.

30

Presidential message, broadcast on every television, satellite and radio network early on 12 January 2049.

"My fellow Americans, I speak to you at the time of the greatest potential threat that this country has ever faced. The acquired immune deficiency plague of fifty years ago, and the massive food pollution diseases that devastated the world twenty years ago are nothing compared to what now confronts us.

"Our very best and latest estimates indicate that any remnants of Adastreia that may escape through our atmosphere are liable to impact somewhere around Virginia. There is also the likelihood of other tiny fragments maybe threatening Germany, China, the Pacific, Brazil and the waters near India. But at best this is mere speculation.

"My security advisers have urged me to leave Washington, warning that there is some risk to my personal well-being—and to the presidential office. But riding the clouds in Air Force One while my fellow Americans face a danger is not my way—never has been my way, and never will be my way.

"You all know what precautions you can take to minimize the danger. I earnestly request you to take them seriously.

"Time is passing swiftly, and these last few hours should be spent with our loved ones. I beg that nobody attempts to break the strict curfew and travel embargo that we were forced to impose in some regions at noon yesterday to prevent panic.

"We are all now in the hands of the Lord, and I commend us all to His keeping. When next I speak to you, this dreadful threat will have gone forever and life will resume its normal gentle patterns.

"God bless America. God bless us all."

31

"The girls?" he asked, not even aware he'd spoken out loud.

"Gone," said a quiet voice.

Dave spun around, the heavy Linebaugh clutched in his right hand, and he saw a frail old man in blue denim overalls under a stained pea jacket. He wasn't armed, and merely stood at the edge of the bushes, looking at Dave.

"Who the—?"

"Wexell. Harry Wexell. Used to be the county sheriff before... Now I'm just old Harry. You're Dave Rand, Miz Bronsky's son-in-law. We met a couple of times when you came up with your wife and young ones."

"Yeah, I remember," David said, holstering the handgun.

"I buried her," the white-bearded man said quietly, looking at the grave. "Didn't have enough to write what I wanted. Wanted to add 'May she run forever beneath God's good sun,' but there wasn't the room. Did the best I could."

Without the least warning Dave dropped to his knees in the wet dirt and started to cry.

THE REALIZATION that the girl's voice he'd heard that night must have been one of his daughters' almost drove him mad. Harry Wexell's account of the gang who'd taken the girls left no shred of doubt that it had been the men on horseback whom they'd hidden from in the snowfall.

"Real giant. Close to seven foot. Name of Sheever. Nobody ever heard anyone call him anything but that. Sheever. Hair like a Kansas prairie in summer. Real cold killer, he was. We figured that some of his mob might have been in the military. Deserters. It was the way they took orders from him."

The old man was sitting around the bright flames of their cooking fire. It was still early afternoon, but the sky was darkening with the threat of a serious blizzard to come. Dave was desperately eager to be off and driving after the gang and his children. But he had first to learn what he could about them and about what had happened.

And the manner of Janine's passing.

"How long were they here?"

Wexell looked at Lee. "You take after your mother, boy. How long? Must be around a month. First off there wasn't much trouble with them.

Fact is, this community lost a lot of people with the quakes and then the cold. So there was plenty of spare shelter and good hunting for everybody. That was the mistake. Your mother could have up and run with your sisters, but by the time she realized...we all realized...what Sheever was like, it was too damned late.''

"Couldn't everyone have got together and—?'' began Zera.

"Not enough, girly. Same as Mrs. Rand. Shake hands with Satan, and you finish up with some fingers missing.''

"Why did they leave, Harry?''

The old man reached out and poked a long stick into the flames, watching it catch and flare. "Illness came, Dave.''

"What illness?''

"Cholera.''

Dave sighed. "Oh, hell. I reckoned that with so many of the dead around, most not buried, it wouldn't be that long before water got contaminated. How bad was it here?''

"Still is bad. That's the reason I'm hanging around up in the mountain. Cleaner. It's taken around half of the folks that survived the Big Hit. They were so weak.''

"And this Sheever got frightened and ran, taking Roxanne and Ellie with him. What about Granny Bronsky? They kill her?"

"No. Heart failure after the big shakes, January of last year. Died the day after your wife got here. It was real quick."

The question couldn't be put off any longer. Dave took a deep breath.

"How did Janine die, Harry? Was it this Sheever who killed her?"

Melmoth pushed against Lee, trying to get himself more comfortable. The pit bull had been quiet ever since they'd reached the house. It had wandered off, and Dave had found it lying, belly in the mud, near Janine's grave.

Wexell took his time answering. He pulled out an antique silver half-hunter and stared intently at it before putting it back in his pocket.

"Don't know, Dave. Wouldn't like to talk about how the body was. Not to you, or the boy. Wouldn't be right."

He wasn't going to say anything more, but when Dave made a strangled sound, he went on. "Wasn't an easy passing, I'd reckon. At the finish I reckon . . . a knife, likely."

"The girls are alive? They with the gang?"

He nodded. "Sure. I saw them leave. I was hiding up behind the barn. Both the girls was crying and sort of comforting each other."

"Yeah, they would," said Lee.

"I'll take a look around inside the house and then we should be moving."

The old man patted Dave on the arm. "Weather's closing in tonight."

"Sure. Start at dawn."

"Where?" said Zera.

Dave looked at her. "How d'you mean? Are you asking where are you going to go? I don't know, Zera. You're welcome to stick along...."

"No. I mean where will this Sheever have gone? By now the trail's two, three days cold. They can move fast on horses."

Dave didn't answer. His simple determination to go after the gang and rescue the girls had only gone a single step forward. Now he had to think about Zera's question. And face the reality that he had not the least idea in the whole country where the tall blond man might have gone. Already he would be close on a hundred miles away.

Wexell coughed. "If'n he's still this side of hell, then I reckon that Hogan might know it. Not that he'd tell you. Little bastard!"

"Hogan?"

Wexell looked embarrassed. "Yeah. One of Sheever's thugs. Got the sickness, and they left him to die. He's holed up in a back room in the hotel in town. Might be dead by now."

"After what they've done...he's on his own and you all let him go on...?"

The old man lifted a hand. "Look, you haven't seen Sheever, Dave. Suppose we'd tried something against Hogan, and then Sheever came back an' found out 'bout it. We'd just finish up like..." He let the rest of the sentence drift away.

"In the hotel?" Dave said, standing up.

"Yeah. The Palace. On Main. Can't miss it. Believe he's in the third floor back. Got windows on two sides. Got some guns with him, Dave."

"Sure."

THE PALACE HAD BEEN BUILT in 1890, hewn from huge logs. Once it had been one of the smartest places to stay for New York's fashionable elite. Now it was close to falling down.

The sun was gone, and flakes of snow whirled on an easterly wind. Dave Rand had insisted that Zera and Lee waited up at Granny's house. He'd taken the Browning and his Linebaugh with him. The old lawman had offered to accompany him.

"Harry, there's some things where a man's got to do what he's got to—and all that. Thanks, anyway."

He walked along the boardwalk, the heels of his boots echoing on the rotting wood. There was nobody around. The swing doors to the lobby of the hotel were open, and he stepped in, finding a wonderful atmosphere of faded opulence. There were crystal chandeliers and overstuffed sofas. The place seemed empty. But Dave's nostrils could catch the faint aroma of marijuana, and there was a light somewhere up the broad sweep of the staircase.

Amazingly he heard the distant sound of someone singing. Very muffled and cracked and sounding like an obscene version of "Shall We Gather At The River?"

The stairs creaked as Dave climbed them. He paused on the landing to listen. Then he went up another flight, the Linebaugh cocked and ready in his right hand.

The singing had stopped, and he heard a fit of coughing. The light came from a half-open door on the third floor at the back of the hotel, just as Harry Wexell had said.

Now the smell of dope was stronger, mingled with the sickly stench of human waste. Dave tiptoed along the corridor, keeping close to the wall to minimize the risk of creaking boards.

Someone inside the room moaned.

Very slowly Dave eased up to the door and peered in. The smell of vomit and excrement was much stronger, and he winced, close to gagging. He could just see the foot of a bed, with some stained blankets on the floor and a couple of empty whiskey bottles.

"Where's the fuckin' whore gone? Gone an'..." The words were interrupted by the noise of violent sickness that splattered on the carpet.

Dave walked in, leading with the handgun, ready to squeeze the trigger at a moment's warning. Immediately, though, he realized from the condition of the man in the bed that the big pistol was superfluous.

One of Dave's aunts had died slowly and painfully of throat cancer, and he'd watched her wither away. He'd seen her in the last day, close to death, eyes blank, her mind locked away inside the shrunken skull. This was worse.

The room was a stinking shambles. The man who lay tangled in filthy bedclothes looked to be around fifty, maybe five feet three inches tall. He almost had no body mass—likely weighed something near sixty pounds, the ribs almost breaking through the wrinkled parchment skin. The face seemed, in the light of a battery lamp, to have a bluish tint, and the eyes had almost vanished into the hollows of wind-washed bone.

A hand, dark skinned, came up off the bed, and the clawed fingers pointed at Dave Rand. "Get some fucking water, you lousy bastard."

The voice was reedy and feeble, yet it somehow still held something of what must once have made Hogan a frightening man. Dave stepped closer, not allowing the Linebaugh to wander.

Hogan's eyes glittered like pearls far beneath a murky river. "You ain't brought water, have you? Finally got the nerve to come and take me out! It's 'bout time. White-bellied fuckin' cowards..."

Dave holstered the gun. Reaching to the other hip, he withdrew the ten-inch carbon-steel blade of the Trail-Master knife.

Hogan managed a ghastly smile. "Prefer a bullet, you little prick. Who the fuck are you? Haven't seen you ... you before."

"No. We haven't met, Mr. Hogan. I'm David Rand. Chartered accountant from Cody Heights, in California. I'm glad to see you're still alive."

"Not for long. Not for ... fucking long. Get on with it."

"Want a word first. You don't know me, but I think you knew my late wife, Janine. And my two daughters." The iron control was slipping, and it felt as if the room were shrinking. He gasped for breath, his knuckles whitening on the hilt of the knife. "Ellie and Roxanne. They'd be sixteen and ten years old. You know them, Hogan?"

"Son of a . . ." The words came very soft, the skinned lips barely moving. "They thought you was dead."

"They thought wrong."

The temptation to ask about the girls was almost overwhelming, as was the need to find out about Janine and how she'd died. But it looked like Hogan wasn't too long for this world.

"Where's Sheever?"

"Gone. He done for your woman, you know. When he said we was going and taking the kids and . . . Jan didn't take to that. Being dropped by Sheever after all she had to put up with . . . Fuck, you don't want . . . your two girls was fine . . . more or less fine."

Dave knew that he was going to throw up. The room stank and visible evidence was everywhere, smeared on the floor and clotted on the bed. Hogan's body was a mass of sores and boils, smeared with his own excrement.

"Tell me where they've gone."

"Fuck yourself."

"Just tell me."

"Gonna threaten me! I'm too close to dying for that, you double-stupe prick." There was a dreadful sound of wheezing laughter.

Dave stepped in closer, tightening his grip on the knife. "Listen to me. I don't care anymore about giving pain. Or killing. I'm not the person I was. I'll do anything, Hogan, to find out where your boss has gone with my children. You believe it, or you don't. Better you do."

The frail figure coughed, a thread of yellow bile running over his chin as he swore again.

Dave nodded. "All right. Let's get on with it." He leaned over Hogan, pinning the man to the stinking bed and holding his head still with one hand, his thumb gouging into the corner of the left eye. Hogan started to yell and wriggle. But by then Dave had inserted the point of the long knife into the socket, probing deeper, impaling the eye.

Even through the red haze enveloping his mind, he was surprised how difficult it was to lever the eyeball out, with a hideous ripping, sucking sound. A little clear liquid, tinted pink, brimmed into the raw, empty socket.

Hogan began to scream and scream and scream.

DAVE CLOSED the door on the shambles. The hotel was completely silent and dark, and he picked his way down the stairs, feeling the stickiness of his fingers on the banisters.

Stumbling, holding himself against the bitter cold, he finally got out to the Bronsky house. Walking into the warmth and light, he saw the shocked looks on the faces of Wexell, Zera and his son.

"Dad, you're..." Lee began.

Dave looked down at himself, and saw that both his arms were covered with congealing blood, clear up to the elbows.

Wexell coughed. "Did...did Hogan tell you where they've gone?"

He even managed a smile. "Yeah. I asked him and he told me. We can get there. Soon as we've got some provisions and gas sorted, we'll go after them." The deadened expression on his face was replaced by one of fierce determination as he looked at the young woman and his son. "We'll go after Ellie and Roxanne. And we'll bring them home."